ARMY
OF THE
DEAD

CHRISTOPHER EDGE

Catnip

For my nephew, Tim

CATNIP BOOKS
Published by Catnip Publishing Ltd
14 Greville Street
London EC1N 8SB

First published 2012
1 3 5 7 9 10 8 6 4 2

Text © 2012 Christopher Edge
The moral right of the author has been asserted.

A CIP catalogue record for this book is available from the
British Library.

ISBN 978-1-84647-145-2

Printed in Poland

www.catnippublishing.co.uk
www.christopheredge.co.uk

A low chanting swirled around the stones, the chorus of voices cutting through the thick chains of mist that swept across the ancient circle. A single word rising in triumph echoed into the infinite blackness of the sky.

Albion.

Scott was pushed forward, stumbling across the frost-bitten earth; shadowy black-robed figures forcing him towards the towering monolith that lay at the heart of the Avebury stones. There, lit by the burning brands that bound the circle, Jerry Daedalus stood waiting.

The politician's face was fixed in a sinister smile and he held out his hand towards Scott in welcome. Around the circle, the Brothers of Albion stood in expectation, their arms raised aloft and the sound of their voices growing stronger with every passing second.

Albion! Albion!

In the shadows, Jason stood over Tom's unconscious figure as Avalon crouched protectively beside her father, a thin line of blood matting his beard. The guards surrounding them were all turned towards the great stone, watching as their Grand Master reached inside his black robes and extracted a long, ceremonial dagger, its silver blade glinting in the moonlight. As Scott tried to pull away, Daedalus grabbed hold of his arm, slicing the blade across Scott's open palm.

'For Albion!' he cried, raising Scott's hand aloft like a bloodied trophy. His triumphant shout was met by an answering roar.

Albion! Albion! Albion!

Daedalus thrust Scott's mutilated hand forward, blood dripping through his fingers, until the torn flesh met the weather-beaten surface of the great stone.

Stepping backwards, Daedalus turned towards the assembled Brothers of Albion.

'Let the Halcyon Days begin!'

As Scott's blood coursed down the pillar, tiny cracks appeared across its surface; grey tendrils of light snaked out from the stone and reached towards the source of their freedom. With a sudden dart of delight, the freezing fingers seized hold of Scott in a deadly embrace, the sound of his screams echoing across the stones.

'Rejoice!' Daedalus told them as Scott writhed in agony. 'Rejoice!'

Their chanting filled the air as the light stretched up into the black night sky; twisting tentacles of energy curling out from the stone towards the edge of the circle as the

Brothers of Albion held their arms aloft in welcome. Then, in a blinding blur of light, the beams raked the circle in a flash of white fire. Cutting through the wreaths of mist, the snaking searchlights sought out the figures standing among the stones. One dark-robed figure after another crumpled with an anguished howl of pain as the beams struck.

Above their heads, a raking claw of light scratched at the stars, tearing a hole in the sky. Through this, the faint outlines of grotesque faces could be glimpsed as they peered down into the waiting world below. A foul stench filled the air – the aroma of the abattoir.

One of the Brothers of Albion crawled forward in panic as the beams ricocheted above him. His dark robes fell open as he dragged himself towards the shelter of a standing stone, revealing the khaki-green army uniform that lay beneath. General Charles Buchanan had served his country well – the crowns and stars on his shoulder a testament to the long campaigns he'd fought in Bosnia, Afghanistan and Iraq – but the terror he felt now was stronger than any fear he'd faced in the heat of battle.

Scrambling behind one of the outlying stones, Buchanan cowered as he watched the dark robes of his brothers being cut down around him. Amidst the tumult, he could see the figure of the Grand Master, Jerry Daedalus, sprawled against another of the stones, his eyes closed against the chaos. In the centre of the circle, a hulking silhouette of a man reached up towards Scott's lifeless body as the monument shone with the light of a thousand suns.

With a thunderous crack, he saw the boy fall backwards from the great stone. As if wounded, the monolith gave out a grinding groan that shook the scattered stones. The hole in the sky began to close and the flickering faces above let out thwarted howls of despair.

Clinging to his shelter, Buchanan watched as the snaking tentacles of light flew back towards the monolith, engulfing the figure of the man still standing there. Nobody could survive such an inferno. The general prayed for the horror to come to an end, but as the last twisting talon of light flailed wildly across the circle, it snapped back towards the outlying stone. Towards *him*.

The man shrank back in fear, but the light was too quick, seizing hold of him as Buchanan writhed and thrashed in agony. Shielded by the stone, the cold hard light poured itself into his open mouth, his nostrils, his ears and his eyes. An avalanche of suffering engulfed Buchanan's mind, obliterating every trace of him from the inside: every thought, every feeling, every memory.

Moments later the light was gone. Crouched in the shadow of the stone, General Buchanan slowly lifted his head. Where before there had been the fearful eyes of an old soldier, two pits of absolute blackness stared out. No whites of the eyes, no blue of the iris – just two impenetrable inky pools of evil.

The monolith stood in darkness. A silence stretched

across the circle, broken only by the low whimpering moans of the Brothers felled by the light. The creature inside Buchanan watched as Scott, Avalon and Jason stumbled down the avenue of stones, their figures shrouded by mist and shadows as they fled. He shook his head, the black pits of his eyes slowly fading back to a steely-blue. There would be time to deal with them later when his full strength had returned. First, he had to raise an army.

CHAPTER ONE

Nearly six months later

Up close the stones looked like sentinels, etched against the skyline. Scott brushed his hand against the towering pillar, feeling the worn grooves beneath his fingers; the ancient stone warm to the touch as though it were somehow alive. Ahead of him, Avalon waded across the field of bright yellow corn, the golden stalks parting as she paced the distance to the next stone. Behind her, yet another monolith lurked at the edge of the field, a weathered spike of stone bathed in the blazing June sunshine, its surface grooved by time.

The Devil's Arrows. The line of three stones lay sheltered below the abandoned A1 motorway, its high embankment fringed by fences and razor wire. Another step forward for the government's grand Greening of the Roads scheme – an end to pollution as the motorways were returned to nature and Britain's green and pleasant land restored. But Scott knew that this was all just a front. He raised his right hand to shield his gaze from the sun, the nagging pain from the scar carved into his palm a constant reminder of the true horror that lay behind the scheme.

Avalon had reached the central monolith now and, turning, began to trace her path back between the stones. In her hands she held a forked stick, the wood twitching with every step she took. Her bobbed black hair was silhouetted against the golden field – the sixth hairstyle she'd had in as many months since they'd been forced on the run.

Six months since the Brothers of Albion had opened the First Gate. Six months from the dawn of the Halcyon Days. Six months since Avalon had lost her father. Six months until the end of everything.

Since that night at the Avebury stones, Avalon, Scott and Jason had scoured the country searching for the Last Gate. They had traipsed round hundreds of stone circles looking for the secret that could stop the Brothers of Albion from opening the Dead Ways forever.

Scott frowned. In all that time they hadn't found a single clue. As Avalon climbed over the stile he called out to her, more in hope than expectation.

'Any luck?'

Avalon looked up, but her dark eyes were filled with disappointment. She shook her head as she walked towards the shadow of the stone where Scott was waiting.

'Nothing.' She glanced down at the forked willow branch in her hand, the bark stripped away to leave the dowsing rod smooth. 'I could feel the lines of power pulsing between the stones, but there was no fracture, no place for the dead to break through. The Last Gate isn't here.'

Scott's face crumpled in frustration. He reached up to brush his fringe out of his eyes, sweat matting his dyed black hair to his forehead. Another wasted day. Another day closer to disaster.

He looked east towards the village which lay in silence beyond the fields; the houses empty and boarded up. The people who had lived there were long gone; no reason to stick around once the surrounding roads and motorway closed. Maybe they could find somewhere there to hole up for the night, Scott thought. Wait until tomorrow before setting off again.

A strange sound suddenly broke the silence – a distant whine like the buzzing of a thousand angry bees.

'What's that?' said Avalon.

The sound was growing louder with every passing second, a shrill jet-like whine that caused birds to flee from the surrounding trees in a sudden cloud of black wings, their frantic squawks filling the sky with fear.

Glancing upwards, Scott saw Jason scrambling down the motorway embankment. His dark scraggy hair, plastered across his face, and the wild look in his eyes made him look more like some middle-aged raver than a detective inspector with the Metropolitan Police. Reaching the fence he pulled at the wire, forcing open the gap where they had broken their way through. Jason beckoned the two of them with a desperate wave of his arm.

'Come on,' he yelled. 'We've got to get out of here.'

Scott's thoughts were racing as he followed Avalon, their footsteps pounding over the scorched earth in unison as they clambered up the grassy bank. Had the Brothers of Albion finally managed to find them? All this time, they'd been so careful – staying undercover, keeping to the shadows, always on the run. But the danger was ever present, never knowing who could be trusted, as the Brothers of Albion tried to track them down. The sinister organisation had already framed Jason for murder and abduction, painting a picture of Scott and Avalon as his brainwashed victims – they would stop at nothing to prevent the truth of their plans coming to light. The police, the papers, the security services, even the government were just puppets, all manipulated by the hand of the Brothers of Albion – the real power that ran Britain.

'What is it?' Scott gasped, as he squeezed his way through the gap in the fence.

Shepherding Avalon forward, Jason nodded towards the motorway, his unshaven features purposeful and grim.

'There's something coming.'

The three of them scrambled through the undergrowth to the motorway's edge. When they had arrived here earlier that afternoon, its six lanes had been deserted with nothing and nobody around for miles. Now though, the tarmac rumbled in anticipation as the shrill whine slowly descended to a throaty roar.

Scott looked up the carriageway. Its surface was pitted

with potholes; weeds forced their way through the cracked tarmac, spiking the humid air. Then he saw them. Two cars crested the horizon, their engines thundering as they barrelled down the carriageway. They were less than a mile away, straddling the three lanes as they surged forwards. As the roar of their engines intensified, Scott saw that these weren't police cars but two maxed-up street cars – a flame-red Subaru Impreza pulling slightly ahead of the white Golf GTI racing alongside.

Petrolheads, thought Scott with a sigh of relief. They'd all heard the news reports about illegal street racers taking to the abandoned roads in defiance of the government's scheme, but this was the first time he'd seen them in action.

Scott felt Jason's hand on his shoulder, pulling him back into the cover of the trees. Avalon grimaced as the roar reached a crescendo, clamping her hands to her ears against the noise. Pulling them closer, the detective nodded towards their own car, a black Ford Focus, parked on the hard shoulder in the shade of a motorway gantry.

'We wait for them to go past and then we get out of here.' Jason told them, raising his voice above the thunder of the approaching tyres. 'We don't want anyone asking questions about why we're here.'

Scott and Avalon nodded in unison. As the evening sun beat down on the tarmac, they watched the two cars flash past their hiding place in quick succession, the growl of their exhausts slowly fading as they burned off into the distance.

Danger averted, Jason led the way through the shade of the trees, heading to the spot where their car stood waiting. As they emerged from the undergrowth, a screech of tyres pulled their eyes back down the road. The white car was reversing, tyres smoking as it shot back towards the gantry.

Scott turned towards Jason, his eyes widening in alarm.

'They must have seen us!'

Jason pushed Scott and Avalon in front of him, urging them forwards as they scrambled over the crash barrier and onto the hard shoulder.

The Golf was only ten metres away, its brakes squealing as it slewed to a standstill in front of their Ford, cutting off their escape. Jason clambered over the barrier, hurrying to reach Scott and Avalon as they stood in the highway.

The evening sun bathed the white car in a dazzling light, its paintwork gleaming as faint wisps of smoke curled from its alloy wheels. The car's tinted windows made it impossible to see who was inside, but as Jason reached Scott and Avalon's side, the snarl of its engine was silenced and out stepped three figures – two young men and the female driver. She didn't look much older than eighteen, with her blonde hair scraped back from her face, and they watched as her boots crushed the weeds growing through the tarmac. Avalon jumped as the doors slammed shut.

'What's this heap of junk doing on our motorway?' the first of the men growled, gesturing with his thumb towards the grimy Ford Focus.

'It's not your motorway,' Scott replied, shaking his head in defiance. He gestured around at the cracked tarmac, the graffitied motorway sign half-torn from the gantry and the twisted metal ruins of the crash barrier. 'This road's been abandoned. It belongs to nobody.'

The man's round pudgy face hardened into a scowl. He stabbed his finger towards Scott.

'That's why it's ours.'

Before Scott could reply, he felt Jason's hand grip his shoulder in warning. The detective pulled him back, stepping in front to shield Scott from the man's angry gaze.

'Look, no offence intended,' said Jason, his voice calm. 'We didn't realise this stretch of road was off limits.' With a nod of his head, he gestured for Avalon and Scott to follow him as he backed away, trying to steer them past the ugly knot of youths to the safety of their car. 'We're leaving now.'

Flanked by her friends, the driver stepped forward, blocking their path.

'You didn't answer his question,' she tilted her head back and gave Jason a hard-eyed stare. 'What are you doing here? Who are you?'

Jason looked down at the way her boots were planted on the tarmac, then met the girl's insolent gaze. She wouldn't have dared talk to him like this if he'd still been in uniform, but the police warrant card tucked away in his pocket was all he had left of that life.

'We're just leaving,' Jason said, making an effort to

sound calm. The three youths didn't move as he tried to step towards his car and he could sense Scott bristling beside him, but it was Avalon who made the first move.

'We're here on police business,' she said. 'You'd better get out of our way. This is Detective Inspector Dyer.'

In reply, the youths just laughed. They crowded closer, hemming Jason in on all sides as he pulled the car keys from his pocket, ready to push through them if need be.

'This is Detective Inspector Dyer,' the woman jeered, repeating Avalon's words in a mocking tone. 'It looks like we've got ourselves a copper.'

One of the men struck out, his hand smacking under Jason's fist so that the keys jumped out and into the other man's hand. Laughing, the man threw them to the driver, who threw them again to the shaven-headed youth, standing just behind Jason's shoulder. Scott shouted in protest, jumping in vain for the keys as the others cackled, but Jason remained still, waiting for this humiliation to end.

'I'm sorry, Jason,' Avalon said quietly, 'I didn't –'

But whatever she was about to say was drowned out by the roar of an engine as the red Subaru bombed up behind them on the other side of the crash barrier. Everyone turned to watch as the car jinked into the far lane, swerving past the burnt-out carcass of a speed camera on the hard shoulder.

The car accelerated again and the youths cheered as it suddenly pulled a raking handbrake turn. The rear-end of the Subaru was slung around as the car swung across the

17

carriageway in a perfect 180 degree spin, before coming to a halt facing back the way it had come. Its handbrake locked, the car's rear wheels spun uselessly against the tarmac, smoke rising from the tyres in warning.

Turning back towards Jason, the girl jabbed her finger up the carriageway towards the car. Even though it was more than five hundred metres away, she still had to raise her voice against the engine whine as its wheels span in ever-accelerating circles.

'This is our kingdom. The government can shut the roads down, but we're the ones keeping them alive – people like me and Dylan over there.' She leaned in so close that Jason could see the beads of sweat breaking out on her skin. 'We don't need any coppers and kids spoiling it.'

The whine of the Subaru's engine reached a deafening wail and the car careered towards them, before screeching to a standstill a few metres away. The car door swung open and out stepped a boy who didn't look much older than Scott, his spiked hair as sharp as his driving. As the others cheered, he raised his hand in a mock salute.

The skinhead turned to Jason with a mocking grin. 'You gonna arrest him for driving without a licence?'

Behind Jason, Scott shifted uncomfortably, his hands clenched into fists in readiness. The evening sun threw long shadows up the hard shoulder as the gang closed in around them.

'Wait!'

The shrill sound of Avalon's voice swung every head towards her. She was standing stock still in the centre of the carriageway. In her hand the dowsing rod, which had been dangling uselessly from her fingers, was now taut and quivering. Avalon stared down at the forked stick and then back up the motorway in the direction it was pointing.

On the horizon a dark cloud seemed to be gathering. Light was quickly leaching out of the sky and the warmth of the day replaced by a sudden chill. Flickering shadows hugged the horizon as the cloud continued to build; dark twisting towers reaching up into a sky that only moments earlier had been a flawless blue.

The still air crackled with electricity and as the darkness of the growing cloud rolled forward, Scott felt the scar etched onto his palm pulse in recognition. He could see shapes in the shadows, grotesque glimpses of decaying faces hidden in the gloom. With a sudden jolt of horror, he knew that this wasn't a storm approaching.

As the smothering darkness slid across the landscape, Scott saw a long black finger of mist reach forward out of the thunderhead and point down the motorway to the place where they were standing.

Avalon turned back towards him, the fear in her eyes reflecting his own.

'They're here.'

CHAPTER TWO

'You've got to get out of here *now*!'

Scott's frantic plea fell on deaf ears as the blonde-haired woman waved her arm dismissively in the direction of the looming darkness.

'It's just a thunderstorm.' She shook her head, trying to ignore the uneasy jitters flickering across the faces of those around her. 'So what if it rains? Give us a chance to try out some wet-weather racing.'

Above them, the overcast skies were a swirling mass of chaos as if the remaining traces of daylight were trying to flee the onrushing tidal wave of blackness. The dark wall of cloud seemed to stretch up into infinity as it rolled down the motorway towards them. Strangely, the skies to the east and to the west were still a cobalt blue, as though the storm was somehow bound to the straight line of the road.

Jason put his hand on the woman's arm.

'This isn't a storm.' His voice rang out in warning. 'We've seen this before. There's something coming through – something dangerous. You've got to get off this road.'

Before the woman had a chance to reply, her heavy-set companion pulled Jason's hand from her arm and squared up to face him.

'We're not going anywhere.' He pushed Jason, the detective's feet stumbling backwards over the cracked tarmac. 'We've heard all these scare stories before – strange lights on the motorways, ghosts haunting the roads. It's all just lies spread by your people to keep us out of the way while you close this all down.'

The man pushed Jason once more and the atmosphere surrounding the group crackled in anticipation of violence.

In the centre of the carriageway, Avalon kept a tight hold on the dowsing rod in her trembling hands. She stared down the oncoming wall of cloud, the swirling shapes rising inside taking on terrifying new forms. The forked willow branch was quivering with tension, its point oscillating wildly as she struggled to keep it under control. A sudden grinding noise shook the ground beneath her feet; the dowsing rod snapped and Avalon let out a sharp cry of fear.

Scott turned to see Avalon's slight frame silhouetted against the rising darkness. As the cloud approached the dense lines of trees at the motorway's boundary, their trunks and branches began to buckle and break; splayed limbs of greenery falling beneath the advancing shadows. The roots of the trees twisted in the earth, as if forlornly trying to pull themselves free before they too were consumed by the blackness.

Scott turned back towards Jason.

'We've got to move *now*!'

Nodding his head, Jason grabbed hold of the shoulders of the man blocking his path.

'My keys!' he yelled in desperation.

The heavy-set youth shook his head in disbelief, unable to tear his gaze away from the towering bank of fog.

'It's just a storm . . .'

A hand grabbed Jason's shoulder and pulled him round. It was the boy from the Subaru – Dylan, the girl had called him. His ice-blue gaze darted past Jason to the darkness descending on them, the danger now painfully clear.

'I'll give you a ride.'

Turning, Dylan sprinted for his car. Jason was close behind, calling out for Scott and Avalon to follow him. The remaining youths stood stock still, their eyes fixed to the sky as Scott darted past them to Avalon's side. She looked up at him through dark frightened eyes.

'Come on,' he told her, fighting to keep the tremor from his voice. 'We're getting out of here.'

They raced towards the flame-red car. Wrenching the passenger door open, Jason slammed himself into the seat as Scott and Avalon piled into the back. The young driver already had his key in the ignition, the engine firing into life as Avalon pulled the door shut behind her.

'Hold on!' Dylan yelled as the car tyres bit into the crumbling tarmac and squealed into motion, accelerating past Jason's Focus and the Golf. He yanked at the steering wheel, the car zigzagging its way past the pot-holes and debris littering the carriageway.

As they picked up speed, Scott glanced back over his shoulder. The swirling mass of cloud was moving quickly now; the shifting shadows skimming the motorway opening up into a ravenous maw. As the car surged forward, the darkness howled. It had almost reached the stranded Golf. The white car looked like a forgotten toy, dwarfed by the mountainous blackness that slid inexorably forward. Scott watched horrified as, from the leading edge of the dark swirling tower, three thick fingers of fog snaked through the sky. They reached down to pluck the car from the tarmac, its white body turning over and over as the fingers tightened their grasp. Then, in one sudden movement, they let it go.

The car arced through the air, wheels spinning madly as it tumbled forwards, before slamming into the motorway gantry that spanned the road. With a sickening squeal, the car smashed through the faded blue sign reading THE SOUTH, tearing it from the gantry in a deadly shower of sparks, before crashing to the tarmac below in an explosion of flames. Beneath the gantry, three small figures ran blindly from the chaos, almost lost in the spreading smoke and shadows.

'Oh my God . . .'

Avalon's voice trembled as she clung to Scott's arm in terror. In the driver's seat, Dylan kept his eyes fixed to the road, swerving past another burnt-out speed camera that had been flung across the carriageway, but Jason's eyes were trained on the destruction unfolding in the wing mirror.

As the swirling dark cliff face surged forward again, Scott saw the three figures clambering into the Ford Focus, still somehow untouched amongst the flaming debris. The car was facing the wrong way – wheels pointing north as the darkness raced to engulf it. The Focus reversed wildly, wheels spinning as the driver brought it round in a sweeping arc, then the familiar old car sped forward with a shriek – accelerating from nought to sixty in seven fear-fuelled seconds.

Scott held his breath, praying that they could escape. Behind them, on the desolate motorway, the burning wreckage of the Golf disappeared from view, engulfed by the swirling mists. However, as the darkness reached up into the sky, the shadows at the summit seemed to be clearing, faint cracks of daylight seeping through the fog.

'They're going to make it –'

Even as the words escaped his lips, the twisted shapes in the mist coiled again. Shadow-like claws extended from the darkness, swiping at the tiny car as it raced forward. The claws raked across the carriageway, gouging chunks out of the tarmac as the Focus swerved to avoid them. Hard left. Sheer right. The shadows slashed down again and again and again until, with one last savage move, a single, clawed finger of fog flicked the car forwards like an empty matchbox.

In his rear view mirror, Dylan saw the Focus slewing towards them. He swung hard on the wheel, pulling onto the hard shoulder, their wheels thundering over the torn tarmac as Scott and Avalon bounced in their seats. Spinning wildly, the Ford shot past them and demolished the crash barrier with an ear-splitting roar of twisted metal and breaking glass.

Dylan slammed on the brakes, staring in horror at the sight in front of them.

The Focus was flipped onto its back like a crushed beetle, smoke billowing out from the caved-in roof. Shattered glass was scattered over the hard shoulder, whilst the jagged edge of the crash barrier speared the car like a hunted animal, its bumper and smashed headlights dangling uselessly in the air. Amongst the mangled wreckage, lifeless bodies lay like broken dolls, their limbs bent at unnatural angles.

Through the crumpled side window, Scott saw the bare arm of the young woman begin to rise.

'Look!'

With a faint flicker of hope, he leaned forward in his seat, crowding Jason's shoulder to point to this sign of life. But as the arm pulled itself free from the debris, Scott saw with a shudder that it was no longer attached to the body it belonged to. From the ruins of the car, the other bloodied corpses began to rise; smashed skulls and shattered limbs squeezed themselves out from the twisted wreck and

25

dragged themselves forward towards the Subaru.

Dylan's hands gripped the steering wheel his eyes fixed on the figures he'd seen rise from the wreckage.

'They're dead,' muttered Jason. 'There's nothing we can do for them now.'

Scott glanced behind at the approaching shadow, his fingers curling in panic when he saw how close it was.

'Drive!'

But the boy sat frozen at the wheel, still staring through the window at his friends.

'Drive!' Scott screamed again as Avalon lunged forwards.

'You've got to save us,' she said, her hand resting on the boy's shoulder. 'Please.'

Without saying a word, Dylan stamped hard on the accelerator and the car surged forward with a growl. The pursuing darkness was now only metres away. It swallowed the wreckage of the crushed Focus, the flailing corpses sucked under an obliterating black tide. As Scott glanced back, he saw grasping tendrils of mist snaking towards their exhaust pipe. The flickering shapes of the grotesque faces in the shadows were grinning now in triumph. The four of them couldn't outrun this. Only seconds left before oblivion.

Directly ahead lay a sliproad, the skies above the junction still strangely blue, but high security fences blocked off this only path of escape, the twisted barbs of wire penning them into this hell.

Avalon screamed as she stared out of the passenger

window, the darkness now all around them. Scott could feel the wall of shadows pressing down on him, the scar on his right hand pulsing with pain as a freezing fog filled the car. He glanced down at his palm as a trickle of blood began to seep from the long-healed wound. He could feel the ice creeping into his veins and his mind fled back to the shadows of the Avebury stones. It was happening again.

In the front seat, Dylan was driving blind, fighting for control as thick fingers of mist wrapped themselves around the steering wheel. He twisted the wheel, the car jackknifing sideways as it accelerated towards the chain-link fence. His foot was pinned to the pedal as the darkness overwhelmed them.

The shock of the impact slammed through the car like an explosion. There was a terrible screeching noise as they smashed through the mesh of steel, breaking free from the black fingers of fog that clawed desperately in its wake. As the shadows cleared from the windscreen, Jason dived across to help the boy grapple with the wheel, the car bouncing up the grassy embankment until it came to a teetering halt against a high hedgerow. Steam hissed out from beneath the battered bonnet as the engine noise slowly faded to silence.

'Are you OK?'

Jason twisted in his car seat, wincing as he did so, to see Scott and Avalon pulling themselves up from crouched positions. Avalon's dark eyes blinked into focus as she haltingly pulled away her arms, which had been folded protectively across her head. She looked up at Scott as he pulled his own hands away from his face, the blood from the wound on his palm now smeared across his jaw. They both slowly nodded and turned to look through the passenger window at the motorway below.

Trapped behind the wire, the darkness was crashing in on itself in a soundless implosion. Contorted faces lost in the shadows as the towering blackness spiralled down into a decaying cloud of dusk before shrinking into oblivion. Low on the horizon, the evening sun shone through the dissipating mist. Nothing but the cracked motorway tarmac remained.

'Your friends . . .'

Jason turned to the boy beside him, but Dylan just shook his head. With shaking fingers he turned the key in the ignition, the engine finally catching at the third attempt.

'Let's get out of here.'

CHAPTER THREE

Scott woke with a start in the back of the car, the dull pain that had haunted his nightmares now jangling again as he looked down at his bloodstained hand. The scar that Daedalus had carved into his palm nearly six months earlier had broken open again. An angry red ravine puckered the pale flesh, grimly reminding him of the events of the night before. The dark shadows swamping the vehicle, icy fingers of mist filling his veins until the car crashed free through the motorway fence. Next to him, Avalon shifted uncomfortably in her sleep, a low moan escaping from her lips.

They had pulled up in a lay-by when the car's petrol light came on, too exhausted to try to find fuel in the darkness of the night. It wasn't exactly comfortable with the four of them crammed in the car, but somehow they had slept. Scott looked at the older boy slumped over the wheel and wondered who he really was. He hadn't said much on the drive here, just listened quietly as Avalon explained the impossible situation they'd just witnessed. No one had asked if he had anywhere else he was meant to be.

Wincing, Scott pulled the tattered bandage that had slipped to his wrist more tightly around his palm. Hearing the movement, Jason stirred and twisted in his seat to face him. His face was as grey as the dawn.

'Morning,' said Scott, an empty word to break the silence.

A sudden clatter outside the car caused both of them to jump, their eyes darting nervously to the source of the sound. Through the windscreen, they saw a fat man in greasy chef's overalls pulling open the shutters to the cafe at the end of lay-by. Beside Scott, Avalon began to stir into wakefulness.

Scott forced a thin smile onto his lips, trying to ignore the throbbing pain digging deeper into his palm. 'I think it's time for breakfast.'

'You're buying – right?' In the driver's seat, Dylan had opened his eyes, turning towards Scott with a hungry grin.

⁚ ⁚ ⁚

'So that's another tea, milk no sugar, and three cokes. Is that all love?'

'And a fried egg sandwich,' Dylan added, his plate wiped clean from the first.

Scott frowned. The older boy's brash manner was grating on his nerves. In the cold light of day, Scott worried that they had told him too much. Avalon had wanted to help Dylan make sense of what had happened to his friends, but revealing the truth about the Dead Ways could put them all at risk. Scott was already wondering when they could get rid of him, but for some reason Dylan seemed keen on hanging around. Probably the free food.

Jason nodded, handing over a grubby ten-pound note and watching as the waitress retreated to the counter and started clattering through the cups in search of a clean one.

The four of them sat hunched in the hard plastic chairs, Scott's elbows rested on the grimy formica whilst Avalon flicked through a discarded newspaper. Their breakfast plates, swimming with grease, lay half finished on the table. Next to Dylan, Jason sat facing them; their table at the back of the cafe allowed him to look out onto the rain-splattered road outside. Yesterday's sunshine seemed like a distant memory, but the images of the dark shadows pursuing them down the motorway weren't so easily forgotten.

'We can't carry on like this,' said Jason finally. 'We were lucky to get out alive yesterday. If that fence hadn't given way . . .' He left the thought to hang there in the silence.

'You mean if I hadn't smashed my Scooby through it,' Dylan muttered.

Scott frowned. Who did this kid think he was – making himself out to be the hero? If they hadn't been there, then Dylan would've been no better off than his friends.

'What else are we supposed to do?' he asked Jason. 'Our only hope of stopping the Brothers of Albion from opening the Dead Ways is to find the Last Gate before they can unlock it.'

'But we've already trekked the length and breadth of the country, searched hundreds of stone circles – Castlerigg, Ringmoor, Dunnydeer, Temple Wood, Stanton Drew and the Nine Maidens – and what for? We still haven't found a single sign.' Jason ran his fingers through his dark hair in exasperation. 'The Last Gate can't be opened until the Winter Solstice – that's still six months away. And in the meantime, things are getting worse.'

'You're right.' Looking up, Avalon laid out the newspaper she had been reading on the table in front of them. 'Things *are* getting worse.'

As Scott reached out and slowly turned the pages of newsprint, every headline seemed to back up Avalon's claim.

FREEZING FOG ON A SUMMER'S DAY . . . HORROR ROAD CLAIMS YET MORE LIVES . . . HOSPITALS OVERFLOWING AS DEATH RATES ROCKET . . . PETROLHEAD TERRORISTS BEHIND MYSTERIOUS MOTORWAY ATTACKS . . . FAMILY REUNITED AS DAUGHTER COMES BACK FROM THE DEAD . . .

'Ever since the Brothers of Albion unlocked the First Gate, the Dead Ways have been weakening,' Avalon continued. 'Through every fresh crack in the ancient cage that imprisons them, the Dead Lords are trying to force their way through. Every day they're getting stronger. These stories are just the tip of the iceberg. The wheel of life is slowly grinding to a halt as the dead return. By the time the Last Gate is opened, it will be an apocalypse.'

Her grim warning was interrupted by a loud hoot of laughter as Dylan slapped the table with a grin.

'Can you even hear how ridiculous you sound?' he said. 'I thought you were just trying to spook me last night with your crazy stories about the apocalypse.' He gestured towards the tabloid spread out on the table in front of them. 'This stuff in the papers isn't real, you know.'

Scott stared at him in disbelief. After what he'd seen yesterday, how could this idiot deny what was happening? But it was Avalon who spoke first.

'I know it might sound ridiculous, but this is real, I promise you.' She held the older boy's gaze and Scott thought he saw an understanding pass between them. He wasn't sure that he liked it.

'So how do we stop the Brothers of Albion?' Scott said, pushing back his breakfast plate back with a clatter and breaking the mood. 'We've got to do something.'

Avalon shook her head, her dark eyes suddenly clouded with sadness.

'I don't know,' she replied bitterly. 'If my dad was here, he'd know what to do.'

The three of them lapsed into silence at the thought of Tom; each of them still carrying their own painful memories from that night at Avebury. The image of Tom's stricken figure engulfed by the throbbing tentacles of energy, the light consuming him entirely until nothing remained in the shadow of the stone.

'What happened to your dad?' Dylan asked, but Scott shook his head as Avalon blinked back her tears. 'Oh, I get it. I don't need to know, right?'

Jason sighed. 'We need to get you back to your family.'

'Don't have one,' Dylan replied with a shrug. 'My dad walked out when I was a kid and my mum's in hospital with my kid brother.' They all glanced down at the newspaper headline about hospital death rates. 'I look after myself.'

An uncomfortable silence hung in the air. All this talk of families only reminded Scott that his mother was still out there looking for him, her head filled with the police's lies about his father's death.

'Was there anything that could help us in *Albion Unbound*?' he asked Avalon. They'd been over this a hundred times, but he had to say *something* to fill the silence.

Dylan frowned.

'What's Albumen Unbound?'

'*Albion* – it's a book –'

'Let's have a look then.' Dylan held out his hand, but the others just stared at him blankly. 'What? You think just because I'm a good driver, I don't know how to read?'

'The Brothers of Albion have it,' said Avalon. 'They stole my father's copy from me at Avebury.'

'Well, why don't you just get another one then? Order it off the internet or something.'

Avalon laughed hollowly.

'My dad spent years searching for *Albion Unbound*. Only a handful of copies are rumoured to exist, flitting behind the pages of history. It's not the kind of book you download online or just pull off the shelf in a library . . .'

Avalon's voice faltered momentarily as her eyes narrowed, then her face suddenly lit up with excitement as if somebody had flicked a switch in her brain.

'The Westcott edition – of course!' she exclaimed.

'What's the Westcott edition?' Scott asked, taken aback by Avalon's swift change of mood.

Avalon turned towards him, her excitement forcing her face into an eager grin.

'The British Library receives copies of every book ever printed in the British Isles, but there are rumours that there are many more that it keeps hidden. All the lost books, fabled texts, occult tomes; the books only whispered about on the edges of myth and history. A secret store of arcane knowledge: the Apocryphal Collection. One of the surviving editions of *Albion Unbound* was rumoured to be in Dr William Westcott's great occult library. However, when the British Library purchased the entire collection the books disappeared from view. That's where we'll find *Albion Unbound*.' She turned back to Jason as the waitress approached their table. 'But how are we going to get to it?'

Dylan looked from Jason to Avalon and rolled his eyes.

'I thought this guy was a copper?' he said. 'Shouldn't that open some doors?'

•   •   •

As the car wound its way from the edges of the city towards the heart of London, Jason kept to the back roads, trying to avoid the main routes monitored by police CCTV cameras. There had been an argument about who would drive, but Jason had pulled rank in the end. Dylan sat scowling in the passenger seat, wincing at every gear change and patting the dashboard when Jason stalled at a roundabout. The city was waking up around them, the pavements slowly filling with commuters battling their way to their jobs and offices.

Scott and Avalon crouched low in the back of the car, still wearing the same clothes they'd had on yesterday. They'd tried to clean themselves up in the service station toilets when Jason stopped to fill the car with petrol, but the rest of their clothes had been left in the back of the Ford Focus, now burnt to ashes on the A1. A fug of stale sweat hung heavily in the air. As the streets slid by, Avalon looked across at Scott who was hunched with his left hand cupped protectively around his right. He'd dressed the wound again, but the bandage wrapped around his palm was stained crimson already.

'Your hand,' Avalon murmured. 'It's still bleeding.'

Scott nodded his head. He could feel the raw ache of the wound, the open scar refusing to heal.

'Ever since last night on the motorway.' He grimaced as a

fresh rivulet of pain pumped through his veins. 'It feels like the shadows are still in me.'

Avalon's gaze clouded over, the pain in Scott's eyes reflected in her own. She dropped her voice to a whisper.

'Just before the crash –' Avalon hesitated, her words filled with sudden doubt. 'I thought I heard my dad's voice.'

Scott turned in surprise. Avalon's eyes were shining with tears, but a strange conviction lurked there too. It had been six months since they'd lost Tom at Avebury, and in all that time Scott hadn't seen Avalon shed a single tear. He'd always thought she was burying her grief deep within, waiting for a time to mourn him properly, but now he realized he'd been wrong. Avalon didn't think her father was dead.

Scott thought back to when this nightmare had first started. Jason had sat facing him then, a look of quiet sympathy on the detective's face as he broke the news that Scott's father had been found dead in his Westminster office. At first, Scott refused to believe it was true, hiding in the expectation that at any moment his dad was going to walk through the door again, alive. Now he knew that could never happen – despite the Brothers of Albion's twisted dream of bringing the dead back to life.

Scott looked at his friend. He would have to help Avalon face up to the truth about Tom.

The car swung around a corner, sending the two of them sliding in their seats. As Scott righted himself, he risked a glance out of the window as the car trundled past the gothic arches of St Pancras station, crowds of passengers milling outside.

'I know what you want to believe,' Scott said, trying to keep his voice gentle for Avalon's sake. 'But that light just wiped him out.'

'That light came out of the Dead Ways,' Avalon replied. 'Not this world, not the next, but the spaces in between.' She looked at Scott, her eyes bright with hope. 'That's where my dad is now – the spaces in between.'

'What do you mean?' asked Scott, still struggling to understand. 'What are the spaces in between?'

But Avalon didn't have a chance to answer as the car turned another corner before juddering to a sudden stop. The traffic ahead of them was backed up, the road's three lanes suddenly narrowing to one. A line of barriers blocked off the nearside lanes as a team of road workers in fluorescent jackets dug a trench along Euston Road.

'We need to find somewhere to park,' said Jason half-turning in his seat as both Scott and Avalon cautiously peered out of the windows. 'We're here.'

Across the street, in the shadow of a Novotel, a high square archway showed the entrance to the British Library and, beyond this, an enclosed courtyard stretched out, shielding the low red-brick building from the turmoil of traffic. A stooping bronze statue pointed the way to the library doors.

'Let's go and borrow *Albion Unbound*.'

CHAPTER FOUR

'I don't care what case you are investigating, Detective Inspector –'

'Davison,' Jason quickly replied, keeping his thumb over the name on his police warrant card before slipping it back inside his jacket pocket.

'D.I. Davison.' The woman seated behind the polished mahogany desk looked up at Jason over the frames of her black-rimmed glasses and pursed her lips in disdain. 'I've been the director here at the library for the past fifteen years, and in all that time I've never heard anything so ridiculous. The idea that the British Library – this country's national archive and one of the world's premier research institutions – has a secret stash of mystical books hidden away. It's beyond belief.'

She gestured dismissively through the long glass window that looked out from her office down onto the cavernous reading room below. The airy white-walled space was split by clean-lined columns and filled with endless rows of leather-topped desks. Seated beneath the arching lights, a small village of readers sat in silent communion, leafing through thick hardback volumes and tapping away at laptops.

'Does this look like some new-age bookshop?' the director snapped.

Jason felt the hairs on the back of his neck prickle uneasily. He remembered Tom and Avalon's bookshop, *Mystic Moods*, tucked away in the backstreets of Soho. They hadn't been able to return since they'd been forced on the run, knowing the Brothers of Albion would be lying in wait for them there. Was there something more behind this offhand comment?

A knock on the office door drew his worried eyes away from the director's withering stare. The door opened a fraction and a pale, wrinkled face crowned with a shock of white hair, peered around the frame. The old man took a half-step inside the room but when he saw Jason, he froze, blinking owlishly.

'What is it Kelley?' The director's eyes flicked from Jason to the spindly frame of the dusty librarian.

'Oh, I'm sorry, ma'am,' Kelley shook his head apologetically, his eyes still fixed on Jason. 'I didn't realise you had a visitor.' The old man's voice rustled like the pages of an ancient tome. 'We were supposed to discuss my proposals for the new cataloguing system.'

'I really don't have time for such trivialities.' The director fluttered her fingers in dismissal. 'You and the other sub-librarians will have to work it out between yourselves.'

She turned her attention back to Jason.

'And if you don't have any other business here *Detective Inspector* apart from chasing fairy tales, then I suggest that you let me get on with my rather more pressing affairs.' The director drew herself to her feet. 'The British Library has thousands of visitors every day and it doesn't run itself.'

Jason looked down at the director's hand held out in anticipation of a parting handshake. The throbbing vein at the back of his neck told him she was hiding something.

'I appreciate your time, ma'am,' Jason replied, taking her hand in his own and shaking it firmly, 'but if you are able to locate a copy of *Albion Unbound* anywhere in your collection, I'd appreciate it if you could contact me right away. You'll find my number here.'

He took his hand away leaving a square of paper with a mobile number scrawled across it in the director's palm.

'No card, D.I. Davison?'

'Just being printed,' Jason replied evenly. The number wasn't his either – it was Dylan's.

The director frowned as she dropped the scrap of paper on to her desk.

'That book doesn't exist, so I very much doubt you'll be hearing from me again.'

Shrugging his shoulders, Jason turned to leave. The white-haired librarian was still standing frozen to the spot, half-inside the office door. As Jason stepped towards him,

Kelley's gaze twitched nervously to the director and back again; he shook his head in silent apology as he backed out of the office door.

. . .

Watching from the bottom of the grand stone staircase that swept up from the library entrance to the exhibition galleries above, the three others spotted Jason as he walked across the plaza towards them, cutting his way through the flow of scruffy students and corduroy-clad researchers that rippled around him. As he reached the stairs, the shake of his head was enough to tell them this trip had been in vain.

'It's no good,' Jason sighed. 'The director's hiding something, I'm sure of it; even if they do have the book hidden away here, she's not going to help us find it.'

'Then what are we going to do?' asked Scott, glancing nervously towards the navy-blue uniforms of the security guards stationed at the entrance. 'There are over 100 million books in this library.'

'Actually, it's closer to 150 million books.' A paper-thin voice caused Scott to spin around in surprise. 'I should know, I keep them all safe.'

An old man stood in front of them, his shock of white hair tipping forward as his emerald-green eyes searched Scott's face. Jason recognised him instantly as Kelley, the librarian he'd seen in the Director's office.

The man shuffled forward, glancing around as he gripped Scott's arms with unexpectedly strong bone-like fingers.

'You're looking for *Albion Unbound*,' the librarian said in a low voice, the scent of dust-ridden books on his breath.

Scott nodded. 'But how do you –'

The white-haired librarian held a finger to his lips.

Pulling at Scott's arm and gesturing for the others to follow, he started towards the sweeping stone stairs.

'Wait a second,' Jason said, unsure as to whether they could trust this strange old man. 'What's –?'

'No time,' the librarian replied shaking his head. 'The books told me that you were coming, but we don't have much time.'

Bustling his way through the students congregating at the bottom of the stairs, he hustled Scott up the stone steps with Jason and Avalon following them closely; Dylan was a few paces behind, glancing around in wonder at the grand architecture. Waving his pass at the security guard standing just inside the entrance to the gallery, Kelley escorted them into a large exhibition space. The walls of the gallery were lined with glass display cases filled with exhibits illuminated under soft white lights. As the old man hustled them forwards, Scott glanced at the cavalcade of books, papers and manuscripts – the Magna Carta, Shakespeare's First Folio, the scientific papers of Sir Isaac Newton – the priceless treasures of Britain preserved under glass.

The librarian stopped at a door marked PRIVATE tucked away at the end of the gallery and, selecting a key from the bunch hanging from his belt, unlocked the door and ushered them through.

'This way, this way,' he muttered, locking the door behind him and leading them down a murky staircase. Scott's eyes struggled to adjust after the airy light of the exhibition hall. Boxes of books, lit by a flickering fluorescent light, were stacked in untidy piles at the bottom of each flight of stairs. At the bottom of the central staircase, five long corridors stretched out in different directions, like a subterranean starfish; four of them lit by the same flickering light, the fifth in darkness.

The librarian stooped as he unhooked a torch from next to the stairs and, switching it on, gestured down the pitch-black corridor.

'Not far now,' he told them, grabbing hold of Scott's arm again, more for security than support, before shuffling forward down the dark passageway.

'I don't like this,' muttered Jason, as the rest of them followed close behind.

'Me neither,' added Dylan, his head bent low as he wrapped his arms protectively round his chest.

'It's OK,' Avalon replied, her voice echoing softly. 'I trust him. He's got a good aura.'

In the darkness, Jason rolled his eyes in disbelief and Dylan smothered a snort of laughter.

Ahead of them, the old librarian wheezed as he shone the torch in front of Scott's footsteps. The beam illuminated the dark corridor as it slowly twisted downwards, taking them further into the bowels of the library. The air around them was cold and crisp and the low humming of a distant generator could be heard reverberating through the walls.

'We're over twenty metres below the city streets, surrounded by millions of books, maps and manuscripts.' Scott felt the old man's fingers tighten around his arm. 'The director herself doesn't know all the books we have. Only I know the books that we have down here.'

'Who are you?' Scott asked again. 'And why are you helping us?'

'Edward Kelley,' the old man replied, momentarily tipping the torch beam upwards to illuminate his pale, timeworn face before sending it flickering back to the corridor walls. 'Sub-librarian in charge of Special Collections. Subordinate, subservient, subterranean librarian.'

His footsteps stopped outside an unassuming door, set back slightly on the right-hand side of the narrow corridor.

'For over fifty years I've looked after this collection,' he told them as he unlocked the door with another key from the bunch hanging from his belt. 'And that's why I'm helping you. The books told me to.'

Pushing the door open, Kelley stepped into the room, pulling on a light cord as he did so. The room was instantly lit by three yellow bulbs that hung down from the low ceiling, each half-covered by a broad metal shade. Scott saw six wide double bookcases, arranged at right angles to the wood-panelled walls, with a narrow aisle leading between them. Books of every shape and size lined the shelves, their pages facing outwards with the spines hidden from sight. Rusting chains hung down from each book connected to long iron bars at the bottom of each shelf. In front of the bookcases stiff-backed wooden benches, like church pews, faced the sloping reading desks at the base of the shelves.

Kelley turned towards them as they crowded through the narrow door, his wrinkled face creasing in pleasure. He swept his trembling hand towards the chained bookcases that filled the room.

'This is the Apocryphal Collection,' he announced, his tremulous voice seeming to rustle the pages of the books waiting on the shelves.

'Wow,' said Avalon, pushing past the boys in her eagerness to reach the books. She stepped towards the nearest of the bookcases, its tall shelves stretching to the ceiling, the rusting chains hanging like auburn tresses from the heavy volumes that lined each shelf. At the end of the bookcase, a single word *Occultus* was painted at the top of the bay and below this a faded index board, filled with an intricately coded list, charted the location of every book on the crowded shelves.

As Scott appeared at her shoulder, Avalon scanned the list, mumbling the titles as she read.

'*De Arcanis Philosophia, The Alphabet of Honorius, Grimorium Maleficarum, The Book of Keys . . .*' She turned to Scott, shaking her head in astonishment. 'These books shouldn't exist – they're myths, legends even.'

The two of them felt Kelley's spidery fingers settle on their shoulders.

'I believe the book you are looking for is this way.'

Tightening his skeletal grip, the librarian led Scott and Avalon down the cramped corridor between the bookcases. The dangling chains rattled as they passed. As they reached the furthest bookcase, Kelley stopped and, from his dusty jacket pocket, extricated a pince-nez which he held in front of his eyes as he strained to read the index board.

'Ah, *Albion Unbound*,' he pronounced the title with a hushed reverence. Shuffling his way to the front of the bookcase, he traced his finger along the shelves, past gilt-edged pages and leather-bound volumes as he searched for the right location. Finally, with a sigh of satisfaction, Kelley's hand reached up, the chains clanking as he delicately extracted a familiar thin volume, its grey leather binding cracked and worn. He reverentially placed the book on the reading desk in front of Scott and Avalon.

'This has the answers you need.'

As Scott and Avalon slid eagerly on to the long wooden bench to examine the book, Dylan stepped up to look over their shoulders. Jason hung back, eyeing Kelley with suspicion.

'How do you know all this?' he asked, glancing back towards the door, half-expecting to see Daedalus and the rest of the Brothers of Albion waiting there. 'Why are you helping us?'

Kelley tried to straighten, his back creaking ominously as he did so. Still stooping slightly, he left the teenagers poring over the book and slowly shuffled towards Jason. The detective watched as the librarian waved his hand proprietarily towards the cumbrous bookcases, their shelves worn and grooved with age.

'For fifty years I've studied these books – keeping them safe, protecting them. Imprisoned within these bookcases is arcane knowledge that's been kept hidden through the centuries – the power and the secrets that only a few have dared to print.' He tapped the side of his temple with a long, bony finger, his papery skin almost translucent under the pale yellow light. 'All mine, safe in here.'

'I know all about the Dead Ways,' he continued. 'And I know about the things that are waiting on the other side, waiting for the gates to be opened. When I turn the pages of these books, I can hear them scratching at the corners of reality. I can smell their hunger as they try to force their way through.' He glanced back towards the others, then grasped hold of Jason's arm. 'I know who you are and what you've got to do. The Dead Ways must never be opened.'

Jason slowly nodded his head, the haunted look in the old man's eyes mirroring his own as he remembered the swirling blackness pursuing them down the motorway, its shadowy terror filling the car with fear.

The clattering ring of a bell made both men jump. Kelley let go of Jason's arm and turned towards the door as the alarm rang insistently.

'Wait here,' he told them as Scott and Avalon looked around in confusion, but Dylan's gaze stayed fixed on the book as he slipped into the seat next to them. 'I'll be right back.'

Silencing the bell on the wall of the room as he left, the librarian slipped out into the darkened corridor. As the echoes of the bell's clamour were absorbed by the ranks of captive books, Jason walked to the reading desk where the three teenagers were hunched over the slim volume.

'Keep looking,' he told them. 'We might not have much time.'

Scott turned back to the chained copy of *Albion Unbound*, its brittle, yellowing pages filled with intricate illustrations of strange ceremonies. On one page, shadowy figures huddled in fear before a circle of towering stones. He clenched his teeth as the wound on his palm throbbed in recollection.

Avalon's eyes skittered over the archaic text as she turned the pages, desperately trying to find something that could help them. Dylan just shook his head in disbelief, fascinated that this thing even existed. The same cryptic warnings of the apocalypse that would be unleashed if the Dead Ways were ever opened leapt from the pages. But as Avalon turned the next leaf of fraying parchment her eyes widened – where in her father's copy of the book there had only been a scorched and illegible page, there was now a vivid painting framed by a border of intricately-lettered text.

The painting showed a young woman dressed in a flowing white robe, her arms outstretched towards the reader and in her hands a shining light. The woman's face was beautiful, but marked by a strange sadness. Around her was a wall of fallen stones, as though she was trapped in some kind of cave or chamber. The words bordering the picture described the secret it portrayed.

'What is it?' asked Scott, his voice rising in excitement. 'Does it tell us where the Last Gate is?'

Avalon shook her head, her lips moving silently as she tried to decipher the faded text.

'It says it shows Albion's last hope – a weapon that can be used to defeat the dark spirits if anyone ever tries to open the Dead Ways again.'

Dylan stared at the picture. The vivid painted lines almost pulsated with an unnatural energy, the glowing light held in the woman's hand shimmering as her sad eyes seemed to bore right out of the page to meet his gaze.

'What weapon?' he asked, almost ready to believe this madness.

'I don't know,' Avalon replied, bending over the desk as she strained her eyes in the pale yellow light. 'The words are almost worn away.' The links of the chain rattled ominously as Avalon tried to pull the book closer. 'But it says where we can find it – the cave at the end of the world, Tregillian Vau.'

His hands resting against the back of the reading bench, Jason wrinkled his brow in confusion; but before Avalon could decipher any more, the sound of hurrying footsteps echoed from the corridor outside.

They turned to see Kelley appear at the doorway, his frail shoulders shaking as he fought to catch his breath.

'You've got to get out of here right away,' the librarian rasped, forcing the words past his trembling lips. 'They're coming to find you.'

CHAPTER FIVE

'Who's coming?' Jason asked, his gaunt features lined with fear.

'The police,' Kelley replied breathlessly, 'They know you're here – the director must have told them. They've evacuated the library and they're heading down here to the archives as we speak. You've got to leave now!'

Jason's gaze flicked back to the book. A familiar hunted look flashed across Scott's face as he looked up to meet Jason's gaze.

'We've got to go.'

'But the rest of the pages,' Avalon protested. 'We've still not found where the Last Gate is.'

She yanked desperately at the chain securing the book to the shelves, its rusting links grating in protest.

'Don't!' squealed Kelley. The librarian's face was ashen as the chain held firm.

'Here! Hold it open on the desk.' Dylan pushed the book so the spine splintered and the pages fell flat.

'What are you doing?' Jason hissed, as the faint sound

of footsteps echoed up the corridor. 'We don't have time.'

Dylan pulled out his phone and the flash fired as he took a photo of the page that Avalon had been studying. Catching on, she flipped the pages of the book as Dylan snapped away, capturing them on his phone.

Jason's hand grabbed hold of his shoulder.

'Come on – we've got to go.'

Avalon cast a despairing glance back at the dusty volume, still chained to the shelf, as Jason led them out through the narrow aisle between the bookcases. At least they had something – thanks to Dylan's quick thinking. As they reached the door, Kelley grabbed hold of Scott's arm.

'This way,' he hissed, turning right into the darkened corridor and pushing Scott ahead of him. With no torch to guide them, Scott kept his hand against the cold surface of the wall, stumbling slightly as Kelley hurried them forward. Darting a backward glance, Jason saw three torch beams heading towards the room they had just left and heard the familiar thump of police boots echoing up the corridor. He knew the routine: search, locate and isolate. They'd hunt through every inch of this place until they tracked them down.

'Hurry,' Kelley's wheezing voice urged them on through the darkness. Ahead of them, the corridor came to an end and the faint outline of a low door was just visible, half obscured by stacks of boxes. Catching his breath, the librarian shoved the boxes to one side and pressed a button on the small panel he'd uncovered on the wall. The door slid open to reveal a cramped service lift.

'Get in,' he told them.

'You must be joking,' hissed Avalon. 'We'll never all fit in there.'

'You don't have a choice,' Kelley whispered in reply. The sound of barked orders and the crackle of radio static echoed up the corridor. 'The lift will take you to the Conservation Centre – it's a controlled environment where they restore the rarest and most fragile books. There's no way the director would let a squadron of police tramp their size-12 boots through there. From there you should be able to follow the fire exit that leads out onto St Pancras station.' He glanced at the faint glow from his watch in the darkness. 'It's almost rush hour – they'll be thousands of commuters out there.'

Jason nodded. It was the only chance they had.

'Come on.' He gave Avalon a nudge of encouragement towards the lift door.

Muttering angrily under her breath, Avalon climbed into the cramped lift with Scott following close behind. As he crouched down, Scott winced as his bandaged hand banged against the wall of the lift.

'You too,' Jason told Dylan.

'No way.' The boy shook his head as he backed away from the opening. 'I can't get in there. I really can't.' In the half-light spilling from the lift, Dylan's face was a ghostly grey. 'Let me take my chances with the police. I'll be all right, I'm not part of this, remember?'

Jason frowned. It went against everything he believed in to leave the boy here. He knew what the Brothers of Albion were capable of.

Swallowing hard, Dylan pressed his phone into Jason's hand.

'Here, take this. With the pictures I took, you've got what you came for.'

The thump of police boots was growing louder, torch beams waving down the corridor towards them.

'Hurry up,' Kelley hissed.

There was no time to argue. Jason took the phone and in return handed Dylan the keys to his car.

'Take care of yourself,' he told him.

Turning back to the lift, Jason folded himself into the narrow space, his arms and legs bent awkwardly as he tried to fit inside the door.

Avalon waved sadly to Dylan and Scott met his gaze.

'Don't give them what they want,' he said.

'As if I would!' Dylan grinned and Scott smiled back as Kelley leaned forward, the outline of his face silhouetted in the gloom.

'Good luck – I pray to God you can stop them.'

The librarian slid the door shut with a clang, sealing the three of them inside. They heard the grinding sound of the lift gears and then the lift began to slowly judder its way upwards from the bowels of the library.

In the darkness, Scott breathed deeply. His face was pressed against smooth steel, the wall of the lift vibrating as it rose.

'When we reach the Conservation Centre,' said Jason, his hushed voice painfully loud in the cramped lift, 'stay close to me. Here, Avalon, keep this safe.'

He handed her Dylan's phone, trying not to think what might happen to the boy when the Brothers of Albion caught up with him.

The lift shuddered to a halt, a thin sliver of light visible in the gap between the door and the wall. In the room beyond, silence waited. It was time to face their fears.

'Remember – stay close,' Jason whispered.

He slid the door open and clambered out of the lift, his limbs cracking as he straightened. Scott and Avalon quickly followed him.

They were standing in a long low-ceilinged room, its pristine white walls stretched past rows of desks on which peeling leather-bound volumes and strange mechanical contraptions rested. From the ceiling the faint hum of an air conditioning unit could be heard, but the room itself was silent. No sign of any library staff, or the police who were searching for them.

In the far corner of the room, Scott spotted a set of double doors beneath a green sign reading FIRE EXIT with a white arrow and the figure of a running man.

'Over here,' Scott started towards the door. If Kelley was telling them the truth, this was the only safe way out. Just before he reached the doors, Jason roughly brushed past him, holding up a warning hand.

'Wait,' he growled in a low whisper. 'Remember what I told you. There could be half the Metropolitan Police Force waiting for us on the other side of that door.' His eyes flicked from Scott to Avalon. 'I want you both to follow me in absolute silence. Not a sound.'

Turning back to the door, Jason took a deep breath as he rested his open palm against the cold steel. He pushed against the door, the heavy hinges squealing as it slowly opened. Wincing at the sound, Jason craned his neck around the door to look out into a brightly-lit stairwell. There was nobody there. Stepping through, he paused and listened intently. From the bottom of the stairwell came the faint sound of passing traffic and the rumble of trains.

Jason gestured for Scott and Avalon to follow him as he slowly led them down the stairs, moving with stealthy footsteps past each landing, every step taking them closer to their escape.

As they reached the bottom of the stairs, another set of steel fire-doors barred their path, a small square window of reinforced glass allowed them a glimpse of the street outside. Scott stepped forward, but Jason held out a restraining hand.

'Wait,' he hissed. 'We're not out of this yet.'

Pressing his face against the glass, Jason peered through the window. The street outside was filled with people, grim-faced commuters with shirt sleeves rolled up, shoppers laden with brightly-coloured bags, all streaming towards the railway station. No sign of the police.

Waiting impatiently, Avalon turned to Scott.

'We had the book,' she whispered, her face still flushed with frustration. 'There were so many things I had never seen – it could have told us so much.'

Scott shook his head.

'Let's just hope that Dylan photographed the right pages,' he whispered in reply.

Jason turned away from the window.

'The coast is clear. Come on.'

Pushing the fire doors open, they slipped out into the busy street, a steady stream of commuters flowing around them. Rain was starting to fall and the sound of police sirens wailed in the distance as the three of them turned towards the station.

'Stop! Police!'

The shout rang out down the street.

Half turning, they saw two policemen, their tasers raised, running towards them from the shadow of the library. As Avalon stood there in shock, she saw the nearest of the officers take aim with his taser, its barrel pointing straight at her.

She felt Scott's hand on her arm, dragging her sideways

into the crowd of frightened commuters who were surging forward, eager to get away from the trouble. On the periphery of her vision she saw Jason, his mouth wide as he shouted a single word of warning.

'Run!'

CHAPTER SIX

As they darted into the frantic crush of commuters, Scott heard a stuttering hiss followed almost instantaneously by a shrill shriek. Glancing back in alarm, he saw the businessman he'd just pushed his way past collapse to the ground, his body convulsing in agony. Only metres behind, the pursuing police officer cursed as he took aim once again.

'Come on!' Scott tightened his grip on Avalon's arm as they fought their way through the flood of people. 'Move!'

As the taser fired again, the crowd recoiled in fear and Scott stumbled forward. Behind him, he heard the policeman bark into his radio – 'Urgent backup required' – as the crowd closed around them.

Jason was only a few steps ahead, the three of them desperately trying to disappear into the midst of the mob as the wail of police sirens grew louder. The relentless tide of people surged towards the gleaming glass entrance of St Pancras station, desperate to find sanctuary there.

Swept past the line of black cabs waiting by the station, Scott tripped, his fingers losing their hold on Avalon's arm as the thunder of footsteps around him quickened. Fighting his way to his feet before he was buried in the crush, Scott hauled himself up against a taxicab, his palms pressed against its bonnet to steady himself against the buffeting tide of people.

He could see the fleeing crowd funnelling into a crush trying to get through the narrow station entrance. Commuters were pinned to the glass as they fought to escape, the chaos of the crowd quickly turning into mayhem. Scott frantically scanned the bobbing sea of heads, searching for Avalon and Jason. There was no sign of them anywhere.

In desperation, he launched himself back into the flood of people. The crush closed around him, people screaming in panic as they fought for breath. Scott felt his leg smack painfully against one of the steel bollards shielding the entrance as the crowd surged forward again. As soon as he was pushed through the station entrance, Scott felt the melee slacken around him; the crowd began to thin out across the concourse, freed now from the jam outside.

'Scott!'

At the sound of his name he turned, twisting his neck to catch a glimpse of Jason and Avalon sheltering in a coffee shop doorway. Scott wove his way through the throng until at last he was standing next to them again. Above their heads, the arching glass roof bathed the station concourse in sunlight, the shops and bars crowded with people, escalators reaching up to the Eurostar platforms above. Fanning out across the station they could see a line of police in bulletproof vests, tasers drawn, stalking through the crowds in search of their prey.

'They'll have every exit covered,' said Jason. 'There's no way out of here.'

Outside, the sound of sirens reached a crescendo; the net cast by the Brothers of Albion was closing in around them. Scott jabbed his finger towards a sign for the Underground, the arrow pointing down the concourse. The crowds were pouring through the entrance like water escaping through the cracks, finding the quickest way out.

'We don't go out,' he told them, his face grim with determination. 'We go down.'

Glancing back at the line of police, Jason nodded and beckoned for Scott and Avalon to follow him. He threaded his way through the edge of the crowd, darting between pillars to screen them from the searching police. The entrance for the tube was only metres ahead, the blue sky behind the station's soaring roof giving way to the strip-lighted glare of the Underground as a wide walkway opened up to the left of them.

Turning the corner, Scott's heart thudded in his chest as he glimpsed another policeman prowling the concourse in front of the tube barriers. Lines of commuters were milling around the gates, touching travel cards to the barriers then slipping through in single file as the gates momentarily swished open. To the left of the ticket machines, two more policemen were standing guard, radios held against their ears as they scanned the crowd.

Jason grabbed hold of Scott and Avalon, pulling them back behind a pillar. A frown furrowed the detective's face as his eyes hunted for a way past. Over the tannoy, he heard a faint hiss followed by the announcement, '*Will Inspector Dyer contact control.*' Both Scott and Avalon turned to stare at him in shock.

Jason felt the anger rising in his throat. He could imagine Detective Chief Inspector Nicholls leaning over the microphone in the control room. The Brothers of Albion were mocking him, trying to force him into the open. His frown settled into a hard-eyed expression of resolve. He wouldn't let them win.

Peering round the pillar, he saw a large group of tourists, identical 'I ♥ London' T-shirts pulled over their spreading waists, clustered around the tube attendant who was manning the wide-access barrier gate. Their piles of suitcases littered the floor as shuffling lines of commuters tutted their way past. Dark patches of sweat were visible under the attendant's arms as he tried to usher the first of the tourists, a dumpy woman with bleached blonde hair through the gate. Her friends shrieked with laughter as her wheeled suitcase caught in the barrier, jamming it shut. In exasperation, the attendant pressed his own pass against the barrier so that the gates opened again and, with an angry wave of his arm, gestured for the entire group to file through. The spark of a plan caught light in Jason's mind.

He turned back to Scott and Avalon.

'This is our chance,' he said, nodding his head towards the group. 'I'm going to create a diversion and I want you both to get through that barrier and head left for the Piccadilly line – they'll expect you to go for one of the nearer platforms. Get the first train east and leave at the next stop' His voice was low and urgent. 'Don't worry about what I'm doing, just get yourselves clear. If it all goes to plan, I'll be able to catch you up.'

'But what are you going to –'

Scott didn't have time to finish his question as Jason sprinted out from behind the pillar. He burst through the crowd of waiting commuters and bundled into the startled policeman patrolling the concourse; his momentum sending them both crashing into the gaggle of tourists still waiting to file through the wide-access gate.

The policeman reeled as he tried to stop himself from falling, the shocked tourists squealing in panic as they toppled, their suitcases spilling open across the floor. As Jason pulled himself to his feet, he saw Scott and Avalon darting forward, pushing their way past the flailing tourists and through the still-open gate.

'Hey!' The tube attendant cried out, but Scott and Avalon didn't look back; sprinting through the criss-crossing crowds they headed towards the escalators. Below them, the Underground spread out in every direction, lines heading north, south, east and west. Grabbing hold of Avalon's arm, Scott scrambled past a lumbering businessman who was blocking their path and the two of them ran, racing through the corridor that connected the sub-surface lines to the ones that lay deeper underground.

Behind them, on the other side of the barriers, Jason ducked under the scrambling grasp of the policeman who had now pulled himself to his feet, and sprinted away down the concourse, vaulting over the turnstiles into the second entrance hall. More police were weaving their way through the crowds in close pursuit, their radios crackling as they called for backup. Jason ran for the escalators, catching a glimpse of Avalon's dark hair as the two of them disappeared from sight into the heart of the Underground.

He pushed his way through the stampeding travellers, the crowds surging towards the escalators in a frenzy of fear as the shouts of the police cut across the concourse.

'Stop – armed police! Stay where you are!'

Jason sprinted down the steps, forcing his way through the crush of people. He saw Scott and Avalon beneath him, half an escalator away, as they battled through the jostling commuters. Behind him, angry shouts were quickly turning to panic as the thunder of police boots began to stomp down the steps.

'Get out of the way! Move! Move!'

At the bottom of the escalator, the crowds were spilling onto the concourse, Scott and Avalon caught up in the flow as an irresistible tide pushed them out onto the eastbound platform. Jason was still metres behind them; his path blocked by the crush of commuters as the escalator suddenly juddered to a halt. He was losing them. Glancing to his right, he climbed over the handrail onto the raised platform between the up and down escalators, his trainers struggling for grip on the polished surface.

Behind him, he heard a yell.

'That's Dyer! Stop him!'

Keeping low, Jason scrambled downwards, leaping from the escalator into the throng of people. Fighting his way through the press of bodies, he searched for a glimpse of Scott and Avalon on the busy tube platform. An eastbound train had just pulled in, its doors reluctantly opening as the passengers crowding the platform fought to get on board.

'Jason!'

Down the other end of the platform, Jason saw Scott leaning from the doorway of one of the carriages. His bandaged hand was raised high above the heads of the crowd, frantically beckoning Jason forward.

'*Stand clear of the doors. This train is ready to depart.*'

The jam of people between them was impenetrable. There was no way through. Glancing back towards the escalators, Jason saw a unit of armed police forcing a path across the concourse, the crush of terrified commuters backing out of their way. If he didn't get on this train, they wouldn't let him leave the station alive.

Flinging his arm out, Jason caught the doors of the nearest carriage. With one last shove, he barged his way onto the crowded tube train, ignoring the angry protests that welcomed him aboard.

As the doors slid shut behind him and the train began to slowly pull away from the platform, Jason twisted his head to check on his pursuers. With his face wedged between the train window and the sweating armpit of a lumbering businessman, he saw armed police fanning out across the platform, brandishing their guns as they pushed through the throng of panicking commuters. He could still hear the screams of fear through the glass as the train picked up speed and slid into the darkness of the tunnel.

CHAPTER SEVEN

Scott twisted to face Avalon, his shoulders sagging with relief as the sight of the armed police rushing the swamped platform turned into a blur before disappearing completely from view.

'We got away,' he murmured as the train plunged into the darkness of the tunnel.

Avalon gave a tiny nod in reply. Her pale face was still fixed in an anxious expression. Both of them knew that they wouldn't be safe until they were far away from here.

The weight of the other passengers on the cramped tube pressed in all around them, jamming Scott and Avalon against the doors of the train. Scott bent his neck forward away from the curve of the carriage wall and shuffled his feet to try and create some more space for them, the large, wheeled suitcases of the heavy-set tourist behind him bashing against his heels.

Get the first train and leave at the next stop.

Remembering Jason's words, he glanced up at the tube map pasted above the carriage doors, the eastbound

Piccadilly line dotted with stations – Caledonian Road . . . Turnpike Lane . . . Cockfosters. Trapped on this train they were a sitting target, it would be so easy for the police to be waiting for them at every station. Jason's plan made sense to him now: get back onto the streets as quickly as possible, before the Brothers of Albion have chance to marshal their forces. Find a place to hide and work out their next move.

'Caledonian Road – next stop,' Scott told Avalon, raising his voice over the clatter of the train as it rattled through the tunnels, their bodies swaying as they held on to the sides.

'What if they're waiting for us?' Avalon's dark eyes darted nervously to the passengers surrounding them, as though she was frightened of who might be listening.

Scott shook his head.

'We've got to take that chance.'

With a sickening lurch, the train screeched as if in pain. Scott was thrown against Avalon as the two of them were pitched forward into the packed scrum of passengers. Scott thrust out an arm to steady himself, his hand banging against the glass partition as behind this a young pregnant woman screamed in fear. A metallic squeal echoed through the carriage before the train finally juddered to a halt. The strip lights in the ceiling flickered, fading low for a moment, then went out completely, plunging the train into the dim yellow emergency lighting.

Scott felt Avalon's hand tightening on his arm as she pulled herself upright. Her fearful words cut through the babble of panicked voices crowding the carriage.

'They've got us trapped.'

The voice of the driver crackled over the intercom.

'Ladies and gentlemen, we are currently experiencing a minor delay but expect to be moving shortly.' Avalon's tense fingers loosened their grip on Scott's arm as around them the clamour of voices seemed to calm. Overhead, the main lights in the carriage flickered back to life as the power returned. At this, a relieved cheer rose up from the passengers, but in an instant it turned to a terrified scream.

Outside in the blackness of the tunnel, the pale shapes of grey bodies were pressed against the glass. Skeletal fingers scratched at the train windows whilst flesh-torn faces leered in. Every inch of the carriage was surrounded by the dead, rising out of the darkness like a nightmare.

Scott's heart pounded in his mouth as he stared out through the grimy square of glass into the eyes of a dead man. The mouldering flesh hung from the man's face in ribbons, a web of dried-up veins visible beneath the tattered skin. As Scott looked at him, the man's mouth opened wide, blackened stumps of teeth bared in a sinister grin. He raised a crumbling finger and pointed directly at Scott as beside him Avalon turned to look for a way out of this nightmare. Then the dead man howled – a deep-throated wail that turned the blood in Scott's veins to ice.

Along the length of the carriage, the glass began to crack, doors and windows splintering, as the dead tried to force their way in. Over the intercom, they heard the driver frantically calling into his radio:

'Mayday! Mayday! We've got an emergency situation –'

Then his voice was cut off in a strangled scream as the peal of breaking glass crackled over the tannoy, his gurgled shriek followed by a snapping, tearing sound before the intercom cut off with a burst of static.

The train was in chaos. Those who had secured a desirable seat below the windows at the start of their journey had leapt into the aisle, only to be shoved back by their fellow passengers who were desperate for any kind of barrier between them and the cold dead fingers reaching through the shattering glass. In the corner of the carriage, a middle-aged businessman, his shirtsleeves rolled up in the heat, was holding his briefcase against a window like a shield. As he stood there, his feet braced against the onslaught, a pair of dust-shrouded arms smashed through the glass, their decaying fingers dragging the man out through the shattered window and into the darkness with a terror-stricken scream.

The lights flickered again; blackness encroaching as the train slowly began to rock from side to side. Above the screams and the sound of splintering glass, a low moan of hunger could be heard filling the darkness. Outside, in the tunnel, the dead pressed in.

'What's happening?' Scott shouted.

'We must have crossed one of the Dead Ways,' Avalon replied, her voice barely audible amid the pandemonium.

'The divide between this world and the next has worn so thin that the dead are breaking through.' Her eyes were wide with horror. 'There's so many of them . . .'

The shredded face of the dead man slammed against the glass, only inches away from where Scott and Avalon were standing. Avalon twisted away in disgust as a blackened smear of brains spread against the cracked glass. Overhead, the lights strobed wildly as the train swayed, the forces outside trying to push it off the tracks. Scott and Avalon were thrown against the doors of the carriage, the reinforced glass splintering as the corpse hammered its head against it again and again and again.

Scott grabbed hold of Avalon's arm, pulling her to her feet as she stared in mute horror at the carnage. Corpses were crawling through the shattered windows, their decaying bodies snagging and tearing on the jagged shards of glass remaining, but still slithering relentlessly forwards. From every corner of the carriage, the dead were rising; hungry grins slashed across their mutilated faces, arms outstretched to embrace the passengers.

'We've got to get the train moving,' Scott yelled, slamming his fist into the faceless maw of a corpse which reached for Avalon out of the darkness, the blackened flesh crumbling to dust beneath his blow. 'If we stay here, we die.'

The train was rocking as more of the dead swarmed around the carriages, an army of nightmares trapping them in the darkness of the tunnel. With a trembling hand, Avalon motioned towards the far end of the carriage. There, beyond the screams of the cornered passengers and the grasping arms of the dead, lay the door to the driver's cab.

: : :

Jason sprawled on the floor as the train juddered to a halt. The emergency lights flickered into life as he tried to pull himself to his feet, using the armrest of the nearest seat for support. As the voice of the driver crackled over the tannoy to reassure to passengers about this unexpected delay, Jason looked up and found himself staring into a nightmare.

Behind the windows of the train, the faces of the dead peered in, their rotting flesh pressed against the glass. The passengers' screams were met by the howls of the corpses outside. With an unnatural strength, their fists hammered against the windows, the glass starting to splinter and crack beneath the force of their blows. *Not here*, thought Jason, *not now*.

Hurriedly, Jason forced a path through the jam of bodies. The sound of shattering glass echoed through the carriage; frantic passengers turning in panic as the dead began to clamber in. Pushing his way through the crush, Jason could smell the fear, but he couldn't help them all. He had to find Scott and Avalon first.

Halfway down the carriage, he saw one young woman trapped in her seat, half twisted round to face the crumpled window behind her. Her suntanned face was now pale as a grey mottled hand grasped hold of her neck and a flesh-torn face leaned in through the shattered glass with a snarl.

Jason grabbed a laptop bag from the feet of a nearby businessman and swung it into the ghoul's gaping mouth. The fingers fell from the woman's throat as the dead man's head snapped back through the window. Jason tightened his grasp around the bag, a slick stain of liquid on one corner. The lights flickered as he pushed his way through the chaos, desperately trying to reach the next carriage before the train was overwhelmed. He caught glimpses of shapes in the darkness, hideous tableaus framed by the overhead lights as the moans of the dead filled his ears.

⁖ ⁖ ⁖

'Hurry.' Avalon's shaking voice urged Scott on as a skeletal hand clawed the empty air right next to her head.

The two of them had nearly reached the end of the carriage. Between them and the door to the driver's cab, a ragged band of passengers had barricaded themselves in. Makeshift blockades of heavy wheeled suitcases and cavernous rucksacks were piled against the caved-in windows on either side of the gangway and a family of Japanese tourists defended the precarious battlements against the dead.

As Scott approached, an elderly woman, squeezed into the gap in front of the driver's cab door, brandished her umbrella at him.

'Get back!' she shrieked, her pinched red lips set in a snarl as she unfurled her umbrella, its sharp metal tip waving menacingly in Scott's face. 'You're not taking me yet.'

Scott batted the brolly to one side, pushing his way past the woman as she cried out in despair.

'I'm trying to save us,' Scott hissed through gritted teeth as he grappled with the heavy door. It was locked shut. The train pitched sideways, throwing him off balance for a moment.

By the door, a red metal handle was fixed behind a square of toughened glass. Next to this, white letters on a peeling green sticker read 'BREAK GLASS FOR EMERGENCY ACCESS'. Scott clenched his bandaged hand into a fist and brought it down in a hammer blow.

As the glass broke, Scott brushed past the jagged shards and twisted the metal handle. The lock opened with a clunk and he pulled hard on the handle. The heavy door swung back on its hinges and Scott rushed forward into the driver's cab with Avalon close behind.

Slumped over the controls, the eviscerated body of the driver oozed messily onto the floor of the cab. Avalon gagged as she stumbled over something, glancing down to see the blank eyes of the driver staring back up at her.

'Oh God . . .' The words were choked in Avalon's throat as she fought to keep a rush of nausea from spilling out.

The windows at the front of the train were gone and there was glass everywhere, the broken shards crunching beneath Scott's feet as he tried to drag the driver's body free from the controls. Through the shattered window, he could feel the chill whisper of air on his face as, from the train behind, the moans of the dead grew louder. Dimly lit by the red light of a stop sign, he could see that the darkened line ahead was clear.

Hardening his heart against the grisly scene, Scott managed to wedge himself into the seat next to the driver's corpse, now pressed against the side of the cab, and quickly scanned the controls. Underneath the scattered glass, an array of yellow, green and red buttons studded the dashboard and, to the right of this, a red handle was pulled right back. Avalon appeared at Scott's shoulder, her pale face set in a tight-lipped frown as she looked out into the gloom of the tunnel.

'Can you get this thing going again?' she asked.

'I don't know,' Scott replied. 'Let's give it a try.'

Grabbing hold of the handle, he pushed it forwards, the train groaning into life as it began to slowly edge its way further into the tunnel. The whisper of wind through the window's gaping hole quickly became a breeze as the train picked up speed. Scott kept his hand pressed hard against the handle as from the carriages behind there came a flurry of distant thumps and thuds, the bodies of the dead falling from the train. He fixed his eyes on the track ahead. If he could just guide them to the next station then they might have a chance of escaping alive.

Two rotting arms lunged through the shattered window. Scott threw himself backwards as the death-mask grin of a corpse hung in the air in front of him, black hair dangling in clumps from the broken skull. The train slowed as Scott's hand slipped from the controls and the dead woman reached for his neck with a howl.

A hissing jet of white foam blasted the corpse out through the window. Her hands shaking, Avalon kept the fire extinguisher she had snatched from the emergency box trained on the dead woman's form until she disappeared beneath the wheels of the train with a hideous crunch. Through the window, the red light of the stop signal flashed by and Scott was jolted forwards in his seat as the automatic brakes cut in. Dropping the fire extinguisher, Avalon threw out her hand, clinging grimly to the window frame to stop herself from falling onto the tracks. With a grinding shudder, the train came to a halt.

Scott tried to push the handle forward again but to no avail; the train's safety system failing to live up to its name.

'The power cut out after we went through that red light,' he said. 'I don't know how to get this thing started again.'

Screams still racked the carriages behind. Looking out through the window, Avalon saw a dim light cast into a wider part of the tunnel, fifty metres or so ahead of the train. An abandoned station.

'We're going to have to make it on foot.'

Knocking out the sharp edges of glass from the base of the frame, Scott helped Avalon as she clambered through the window. The screams were getting louder now and Scott shuddered to think about the carnage that was unfolding behind them.

'What about Jason?' Avalon asked, standing on the tracks as Scott jumped down from the cab to the rails below. He stumbled, hearing the warning hum of the live rail too close for safety before scrambling back to his feet. Scott reached for Avalon's arm in the darkness, tugging her towards the dimly-lit tunnel ahead.

'He'll find us.'

Backed against the doors of the train, Jason slammed the laptop into an onrushing skeletal shape, its bones crumbling beneath the blow. The carriage was heaving with corpses, their rotting flesh filling the train with the stench of death. Wiping the sweat from his eyes, Jason swung the bag in a threatening arc as the crush of dead pressed in. He wouldn't be able to hold them off for much longer.

He felt the train judder into life, the carriage suddenly lurching forward. Jason saw the dead who were crowding the gangway stagger and fall backwards as the train picked up speed; their outstretched arms flailing as the whine of the motor rose above their moans. Glancing outside, Jason saw the corpses fall from the windows as they were sucked into the train's slipstream.

Then with a juddering groan, the train began to slow. Jason twisted to face the doors, ready to flee the moment the train stopped. He'd find Scott and Avalon and they'd take their chances with any police waiting at the station if it meant escaping from this rolling boneyard alive. But instead of the bright lights of the platform, he could only see darkness as, with a hiss, the train ground to a standstill.

Glancing back, Jason saw the dead rising again. A stinking corpse lurched forward, his ragged grey skin hanging from his bones like a shroud. Jason swung his weapon with renewed vengeance, cleaving the corpse's skull from its torso with a single blow. He had to get out of here.

Jason rammed the corner of the laptop between the train doors, his muscles straining as he tried to wrench them apart. With a screech of defiance, they slowly inched open and Jason flung himself forward, squeezing through the narrow gap, skeletal fingers reaching out behind him in vain.

Jumping down onto the tracks, his eyes quickly scanned the blackness. At the front of train, he glimpsed two shadowy figures scurrying down the rails, framed in the dimly-lit tunnel.

'Scott! Avalon!'

Jason's shout echoed painfully in the cramped confines of the tunnel and the low moans of the dead rose in reply. Ahead of him, Scott and Avalon turned. With a frantic wave of his arm, Scott urged Jason on. As he stumbled past the train, Jason glanced up at the crowded carriages. He could see the corpses swaying in the aisles – it didn't look like a single passenger remained alive.

As he reached Scott and Avalon's side, Jason saw the

light ahead of them in the darkness. He could just make out the rubble of a disused platform with grimy white and red tiles curving up around the walls, a derelict sign just visible in the gloom. *YORK ROAD*.

Grabbing Scott's arm, he pointed the way ahead.

'There must be a way to the surface.'

The three of them stumbled down the tracks, clambering across the rubble, their feet scrabbling through the debris. Behind them, they could hear the desperate sound of hammering and banging from the bodies trapped inside the train, but Scott knew that they were already dead.

Halfway along the tiles, there was a doorway and faded sign indicating the way out. Beyond this, Scott saw a flight of worn steps reaching upwards, a faint orange glow above the emergency exit sign showing them the way.

'Come on,' he called out, tugging at Avalon's arm.

'Look,' she pointed back down the track. At the gaping window of the driver's cab, a cluster of the dead stood frozen, their arms outstretched as a low moan of frustration echoed down the tunnel.

'Why aren't they coming for us?' Jason asked, frowning.

'Something's stopping them,' Avalon replied. 'They're bound to the path of the Dead Ways – they can't cross over fully into our world until the Last Gate is unlocked.'

'We've still got the Brothers of Albion to worry about,' said Scott as he turned towards the emergency exit and the way out.

CHAPTER EIGHT

Dylan sat slouched on a hard plastic chair, the mug of tea on the desk in front of him still untouched. Fixed to the wall, an ancient tape machine whirred noisily, recording every moment of the police interview as it entered its second hour. On the other side of the desk, two men were seated, their cheap suits making it obvious they were plain-clothes detectives.

The first of the two men looked as though he was auditioning for the bad cop role in a low-budget film, leaning forward on his elbows as he fixed Dylan with an intimidating stare, whilst the second, older man ran his fingers through his thinning black hair with a sigh. On the desk in front of them, three A4 photographs were laid out: the faces of Jason, Avalon and Scott, captured for posterity.

'So, let's get this straight,' Detective Chief Inspector Nicholls, the older of the two, said. 'You've never seen any of these people before even though the CCTV pictures clearly show you entering the British Library with them earlier today.'

Dylan lifted his eyes from the desk, meeting the detective's gaze with a surly stare.

'That's right,' he sniffed.

'And you just happened to be picked up by anti-terrorist officers wandering around a restricted area in the middle of a full-blown alert while the rest of the library was being evacuated.'

'I got lost.'

DCI Nicholls leaned forward, the harsh lights of the interview suite highlighting the bald spot hidden on the crown of his head.

'You're really trying to tell me that the names Jason Dyer, Scott Williams and Avalon Moody mean nothing to you?' A frown creased his forehead. 'Don't you even watch the news?'

Dylan shook his head.

'Nah, that stuff's boring,' he replied, a sly grin playing around the edge of his mouth. 'The only thing I watch on TV is *Top Gear*.'

DCI Nicholls pushed himself up from his chair in exasperation. He'd been asking the same questions over and over again, but he was still no closer to finding out what this boy really knew. What would it take to get the kid to crack?

He leaned menacingly over the desk, his sour-faced profile reflected in the broad mirror that spanned one wall of the interview room.

'If I were you, I'd start thinking fast.' He jabbed his finger at Jason's photograph on the desk. 'This is a dangerous man. Dyer's wanted for murder, kidnapping and suspected terrorism. If you have any information about where I can find him and these poor kids that he's kidnapped, you better tell me now.'

Nicholls waited, but in reply the boy just shrugged his shoulders.

'I don't know anything.'

His features darkening into a scowl, the detective turned on his heel and headed for the door. Opening it, he glanced back at Dylan still slouched behind the interview desk.

'Wait here,' he said. 'I've not finished with you yet.'

DCI Nicholls slammed the door shut behind him, leaving Dylan alone with the other surly detective.

Leaning back in his chair, Dylan couldn't keep the grin from spreading across his face. Whether it was dealing with the North Yorkshire Police or these crappy detectives from the Met, he knew how to play the game. He'd been pulled over by the cops often enough to learn. Just play dumb and keep your mouth shut. Never tell the pigs a single thing. They'd soon get bored and let him go.

His eyes flicked down to the photos on the desk. Jason, Scott and Avalon stared back up at him, their faces instantly familiar. Dylan's gaze lingered on the picture that the copper had jabbed his finger against. In this Jason was dressed in a police uniform, his dark-brown hair neatly trimmed as he stared into the camera lens. He didn't look like a killer, no matter what that other cop said.

Shaking his head, Dylan's mind whirled with everything that had happened to him over the past twenty-four hours. He had seen his mates crash their car in the middle of that crazy storm and then watched as their dead bodies walked free from the wreckage. He'd listened as Avalon told him about the Dead Ways and how a secret society called the Brothers of Albion was closing down the roads to bring the dead back. He hadn't believed her at first, just tagged along down to London for the ride – an excuse to escape the reality of what he'd seen. But that book they'd found hidden in the library seemed to suggest it was all true. He could picture the page laid open in front of him, the painting of the pale lady holding a shining light in her hand. Dylan's brow furrowed in concentration, trying to remember exactly what Avalon had said. A weapon that could stop the Dead Ways from opening, hidden somewhere in a cave and the name of a place: Tregillian Vau.

Dylan tapped his fingers against the desk as the policeman facing him frowned. He couldn't wait to get out of this place. He'd given Jason his mobile, so all he'd need to do was call up his own number to hook up with them again. He wanted to see that picture again, or maybe the real thing. Dylan couldn't stop himself from smiling – putting one over on the cops, going on the run, searching for a secret weapon – this trip was giving him a bigger buzz than racing his Scooby.

From behind the glass of the two-way mirror, Jerry Daedalus stared at Dylan with disdain.

'The boy knows more than he's telling you,' he said. 'You need to get him to talk.'

Standing beside him, his crumpled suit looking worn and shabby next to the politician's expensively-tailored pinstripes, DCI Nicholls nodded his head.

'I've dealt with hundreds of cocky little runts like Dylan Mason before. A night in the cells will soon loosen his tongue.'

Daedalus shook his head. 'We don't have time for such niceties,' he replied. 'I cannot risk the carefully-laid plans of the Brothers of Albion on the whims of some young thug. We need to find out where Dyer and those children are now.'

He turned towards DCI Nicholls, a glowering expression disfiguring the politician's normally smooth features.

'*Albion Unbound* contains the secrets of the Dead Ways. We need to find out what they have read. The librarian who helped them can't tell us anything now after his unfortunate heart attack, but this boy looks as though he's made of stronger stuff. He'll talk.'

Nicholls paled.

'You mean you want me to . . .'

Daedalus nodded, a shadow falling across his face as he turned back towards the glass.

'Do this the old-fashioned way,' he said, a chill tone of command in his voice. 'I want to find them *now*.'

'So where is Tregillian Vau?'

Scott rubbed his wet hair with a towel, the newly-applied blonde hair-dye staining the grubby cream material with large yellow patches. Perched next to him on the edge of the bed, Avalon peered down at the screen of Dylan's phone. Tapping her finger, she brought up a map of Great Britain, and then flicked her fingers apart the screen to zoom in on the south-west corner of the map.

'It's in Cornwall,' she replied, expanding the screen again and again as she zoomed in closer and closer. 'Tregillian Vau is a village ten miles north of Land's End. That's where we have to go.'

Pacing the cramped room, Jason turned as Avalon held up the phone for them both to see. The bare bulb overhead was reflected on the mobile's screen, not much brighter than the light from the lamppost outside as it shone through the thin bedroom curtains. This backstreet bed and breakfast had been the safest place they could find when they escaped from the derelict tube station, leaving the nightmare behind. Any questions the landlady might have had dried on her lips as she got her hands on the last of the notes from Jason's wallet. With a bin bag full of stolen charity shop clothes dumped at the end of the bed, they tried to work out their next move.

Scanning through the photos on Dylan's phone, Avalon had almost cried in frustration; every single shot was too dark, the words of *Albion Unbound* impossible to decipher on the tiny mobile screen. Only the photo of the woman in the white robes was legible, a blurry globe of light held in her hand. Avalon could remember the message written beneath this, the words burnt into her brain.

Albion's Last Hope. A Weapon to Defeat the Darkness that Lurks Beyond the Dead Ways. Find the Cave At The End of The World. Tregillian Vau.

A search using the internet on Dylan's phone had quickly solved this only clue. The place was too small to have a Wikipedia entry, but Google Maps had come up trumps. Now taking hold of the phone, Jason stared down at the screen, the map showing a tiny village nestled on the Cornish coast just north of Land's End. A single road ran through the village, a handful of houses scattered on either side. He frowned.

'And what are we going to find there?' he asked doubtfully, his finger hovering over the screen as it picked out a solitary pub, a church and a village shop. 'It doesn't look like there's any caves there.'

'That's where you're wrong,' Avalon replied as she snatched the phone back. 'There's a fogou.'

She tapped at the mobile screen.

'What's a fogou?' Scott asked, peering over her shoulder as the website of the British Archaeological Society loaded.

A picture of what looked like the entrance to a cave could be seen beneath the words 'Tregillian Vau Fogou'.

'It's an old Cornish word that means cave,' Avalon replied. She scrolled down the screen as she read the information there. 'Fogous were built by the ancients – man-made chambers cut into the earth. Some archaeologists think that they were built as graves or as defences, but others believe that fogous were places where the ancients communicated with the spirits of the dead.'

Avalon glanced up, her bobbed hair framing her face.

'That's where we'll find the weapon to stop the Dead Lords.' Her dark eyes shone with hope. 'At the cave at the end of the world. We have to go to Tregillian Vau.'

A doubtful expression was still written across Jason's features.

'I don't know,' he said with a shake of his head. 'All we've got to trust is a painting from that ancient book. It's far too risky going all that way on what could be a wild goose chase.'

Scott looked at him.

'Have you got any better ideas?'

Jason's silence was answer enough.

'How are we going to get there?' Avalon asked, sliding her finger across the screen to bring up the map again. 'The police will be watching the train and coach stations and we don't have a car any more.'

Her thoughts turned towards Dylan. The last glimpse

she'd had of his face had been in the dark shadows of the British Library as the police closed in. She hoped he was all right.

Untroubled by such concerns, Scott stuck out his thumb with a grin.

'We hitchhike,' he replied.

⁙

'That's all I know, I promise you,' Dylan sobbed, a line of blood trailing from his mouth. A legion of cuts and bruises covered his face, his right eye almost swollen shut as he looked up at DCI Nicholls through frightened eyes. He spat out another broken shard of tooth. 'Please let me go,' he begged.

DCI Nicholls raised his eyebrows.

'Are you sure that's all you know,' he sneered. 'I mean, you said that before and all it took was a little encouragement from Detective Sergeant Wilson here to jog your memory.'

He gestured towards the burly figure of the second policeman looming over Dylan. The forensic gloves the plainclothes policeman had pulled over his hands for the interrogation were covered in blood. Dylan cried out in fear.

'Please don't let him hurt me again!'

Sobbing, he buried his head in his hands.

Tapping his colleague on the arm, DCI Nicholls gave a nod and the two men stepped across towards the door of the interview room.

'I'll finish things up here,' Nicholls said as he opened

the door for DS Wilson to step through. 'You go and get yourself down to the pub.'

The second policeman grinned.

'Cheers, guv.'

As Wilson left, Nicholls locked the door behind him with a click. He turned back towards Dylan, still slumped against the interview table, the tape recorder on the wall now silent.

'I'm glad you decided to come clean in the end,' he said as he walked back to the desk.

Dylan raised his head.

'You'll let me go now?' he asked, his voice still trembling in fear.

DCI Nicholls rested his hand on the boy's shoulder.

'Why wouldn't I,' he replied. 'After all, you've told me everything that you know. You've been most useful to us Dylan.' Nicholls's hand slipped down to Dylan's throat. 'But I can't risk you telling anyone else.'

Wrapping his other hand round Dylan's throat, DCI Nicholls tightened his grip. Dylan gasped, his face turning purple as he fought for breath. His legs drummed against the bottom of the desk, thrashing wildly as he tried to break free.

'Please . . .'

But the detective was too strong. Keeping his fingers clamped around Dylan's throat, he stared grimly ahead until eventually the drumming stopped and, with a gurgle, the boy went limp in his arms. Releasing his grip, Dylan's head slumped against the desk, his cold dead eyes staring sightlessly into the beyond.

DCI Nicholls glanced up at the mirror on the wall. Behind it, Jerry Daedalus watched him with a grim smile of satisfaction.

'They're heading for Tregillian Vau.'

CHAPTER NINE

'You've picked a rotten day for hitchhiking.' The elderly woman leaned forward in the driver's seat, peering past the windscreen wipers as they battled against the rain. Her greying hair was piled like a bird's nest on top of her head, whilst a long scarf was coiled around her neck to keep out the cold. As she pulled back out into the river of traffic thundering down the A33, she glanced across at Jason in the passenger seat beside her. 'Are you all heading off on your holidays?'

'Er, yes,' Jason stuttered in reply. His mind struggled to keep pace with his mouth as he improvised. 'I'm taking them down to Cornwall to spend the school holidays with their mum.' Glancing back in the mirror, he saw Scott and Avalon in the backseat raise their eyebrows in surprise.

'Ah, that's nice,' the woman beamed in reply. 'I like the idea that I'm bringing a family together. You've got to help others in this life, haven't you?' She flicked up the indicator as the Fiesta slipped into the fast lane, the car's heater whirring asthmatically against the British summer. 'My daughter's always telling me to stop giving lifts to hitchhikers – she reads me these terrible stories from the newspapers – but like I tell her, I like the company.'

In the back of the car, Scott shivered as the rainwater slowly seeped through his clothes, running down in freezing rivulets and pooling around his feet. He stared down at his sodden trainers, the water staining the discarded newspaper beneath them. Scott froze as he glimpsed the headline smeared under his feet.

SIX MONTHS ON: MOTHER PLEADS WITH 'KILLER' GIVE ME BACK MY SON

Beneath this headline, he saw a photo of his mum, her face streaked with tears as she stared out of the sodden newsprint. Numbed, Scott's eyes rolled down the column of text next to the picture.

At an emotional police press conference yesterday, the ex-wife of murdered civil servant Alexander Williams pleaded again with her husband's suspected killer, rogue cop Jason Dyer, to release her son Scott, unharmed. Flanked by DCI Eddie Nicholls, the detective leading the enquiry, Madeleine Phillips, 39, sobbed as she begged her son's abductor to set him free. 'He's my only child and I can't live without him. It's been nearly six months, but I believe with all my heart that Scott's still alive . . .'

Continued on page 3.

The words swam in front of Scott's eyes. Every single day he'd tried to put all thought of his mum to the very back of his mind; he'd convinced himself that it was safer that way. If she didn't know where he was, then the Brothers of Albion wouldn't be able to use her to find him. But now he could see their hands behind this story, taunting him through the torn newsprint.

He fought to keep his emotions in check, angrily twisting his foot so that the waterlogged page crumpled and tore, then pushing it forward out of sight. The glimpse of his mum's tear-stained face had torn open the scab that had hardened around his heart. He wanted to phone her – tell her that he was safe and warn her about what was really going on. But he knew that the Brothers would be listening on the other end of the line, ready to hunt him down. And if they did . . .

Scott turned to look through the window, the rain running in horizontal streaks across the glass as the rumbling asphalt flashed by under a slate-grey sky. He couldn't call her. He wasn't safe; nobody was.

The midsummer solstice was three days away. Half the year nearly gone and only six months left until the Brothers of Albion unlocked the Dead Ways forever. Scott shivered at the thought of what was waiting on the other side; the ravenous hunger of the Dead Lords longing to feast on the living. They had to get to Tregillian Vau and find the secret weapon that the ancients had hidden there.

He glanced across at Avalon whose head was already resting against the glass. Scott felt his own eyes growing heavy. They'd been running from danger for so long. Now, as exhaustion overtook him and he slowly slipped into an uncomfortable sleep, the thoughts of what could be waiting for him in the depths of Tregillian Vau crowded his dreams.

Scott woke with a shudder. The side of his face was numb as he peeled it away from the glass. Outside the rain still hammered down, bouncing off the tarmac as the traffic around them slowed to a crawl. He caught sight of a large blue sign by the roadside, its stark white letters announcing DEVON LINK ROUTE UPGRADE – GREENING YOUR JOURNEY and beneath this in smaller letters DELAYS EXPECTED. Blearily wiping the sleep from his eyes, Scott turned forward to see Jason hunched in the passenger seat, his shoulders bent as if worn down by the incessant jabbering of the grey-haired woman beside him.

'Dear, oh dear,' she tutted as the Fiesta finally came to a halt. On the road in front of them the traffic had come to a standstill, brake lights flashing red as long lines of fluorescent cones funnelled the cars into stationary queues.

'I thought we'd have got to Exeter by now – it'll be your best chance of finding another lift to take you all the way down to Cornwall – but with these roadworks, I really don't know.' She tapped her fingers against the steering wheel impatiently.

'I'm all for the environment of course, but we've not seen half of these Maglev trains they promised us to replace all of the roads and motorways they've dug up. I swear the traffic's getting worse not better.'

Glancing across at Scott, Avalon raised her eyebrows in response to the driver's words. If only she knew.

'I remember when I could make this drive down to Devon in less than four hours, but nowadays –'

The woman paused, her fingers suddenly tightening around the wheel and a strange strangled sound emanated from the back of her throat.

Jason looked across in alarm to see the old woman's hands scrabbling at her face, her red lipstick bright against her waxen skin. She turned towards him, her frightened eyes freezing into a glassy-eyed stare.

'I'm – I'm – I'm –'

The words came from the woman's lips in tight little gasps, her voice straining to make a sound. She shook her head violently, jewellery rattling in protest and then her head slumped forwards, hanging motionless between her shoulders.

Jason reached out in panic, his hands trying to loosen

the haberdashery of scarves swaddled around the woman's withered neck. He twisted to face Scott and Avalon.

'I think she's had some kind of fit!'

The woman's arm shot up and swatted Jason's hands away. He reeled back in surprise as she slowly turned to face him, her neck swivelling in a series of tiny jerks as if manipulated from within by pulleys and levers. The old woman's eyes were still frozen into an unsettling stare as she jerkily raised her hands in front of her face. She turned them slowly as if oddly fascinated by the sight of the wrinkles criss-crossing in lines and dark brown liver spots staining the skin.

'Are you OK?' Jason asked, anxiously leaning forwards as her hands suddenly dropped to her lap.

'I didn't think I was going to make it.'

The old woman's voice seemed strangely altered, a deep rumble of words that rasped in the back of her throat. She twisted around in her seat, her upper body moving in reluctant jerks as she turned to face Scott and Avalon.

Scott stared at the old woman in horror as her eyes rolled up in her head and her quivering lips moved to form the words:

'Avalon, Scott – I didn't think I'd get to see you again.'

'How do you know our names?' Scott breathed, the thought of the newspaper headline crumpled beneath his feet fuelling his fear.

But Avalon was already leaning forward, her dark eyes

shining with hope as she reached a hand out to touch the woman's face.

'Dad,' she asked. 'Is that you?'

The old woman's head jerked once in reply.

'I had to find you, Avalon.' The rumbling tone seemed to echo Tom's. 'I had to find you all to warn you.'

'What?' Jason spluttered. He looked from Avalon to the old woman, her greying bird's nest hair still piled on top of her head, then back to Avalon again. 'You're trying to tell me that this is Tom?'

The old woman turned, fixing her white-eyed stare on Jason as her mouth fell open in a crooked smile.

'Hello D.I. Dyer.' The words rasped from her lips. 'Thank you for keeping them safe.'

Jason blinked, slowly shaking his head in denial. They'd all seen the same sight six months ago, the blazing light that had obliterated the bookseller. Only Avalon remained unsurprised.

'I knew it!' Avalon slapped her palm against the car seat in excitement. 'I told them that you couldn't be dead. They wouldn't believe me, but I knew.'

'You're right. My body was wiped out, but my soul survived.'

Tom's voice was growing stronger now as the old woman uttered his words.

'And that light, it took me inside the Dead Ways. I could see everything. All human consciousness: the living and the dead, all pulsing in endless pathways stretching out across the astral planes. I could go anywhere, do anything, know everything. All this time I've been searching, trying to find a way to stop them from opening the Dead Ways for good.'

'You're going to help us? You've found a way back?'

Avalon's words hung in the air as the old woman's head shook slowly, strands of grey hair falling across her lifeless eyes.

'I can channel my spirit into this woman's body for a short time, but my own body was destroyed at Avebury.' Tom's voice faltered in the old woman's throat. 'I can't come back.'

Avalon's face crumpled in pain.

'But you've got to come back,' she pleaded, running her fingers through her hair in frustration. 'We've got to stop the Brothers of Albion from opening the Last Gate – we can't find it without you.'

A single tear rolled down the creases in the old woman's face, her eyes still blank and set in a glassy-eyed stare.

'I'm sorry.'

As Avalon slumped back defeated, Scott leaned forward in his seat.

'But you've got to help us. We're heading down to Cornwall now to look for some fabled weapon that can stop the Dead Lords and we don't even know what it is.'

'I came here to warn you.' The sound of Tom's voice was strangely unsettling as it rumbled from the old woman's pinched red lips. 'The Dead Lords know what you're doing – that you're trying to stop the Dead Ways from being opened. They're searching for you too.'

'You mean the Brothers are?' Scott reached down, pulling the sodden newspaper from the floor and brandishing its torn headline.

'I mean the Dead Lords.'

'I thought they were still caged on the other side of the Dead Ways?' said Scott asked, the taste of fear suddenly rising in his throat.

The woman's face twitched from side to side.

'The opening of the First Gate let them halfway through. They're trapped here in the Dead Ways with me. When I crossed over, my consciousness was observed, all my memories – how we were trying to stop the Brothers of Albion from opening the Dead Ways – they could see it all. And I could see them . . .'

The old woman's voice trailed into silence, a sliver of spittle hanging from her bottom lip. When she started to speak again, her voice sounded thin and stretched like cellophane.

'The Dead Lords are tired of waiting for the winter solstice, for the last lock to be opened so they can feast on the souls of the living once again. They've sent an emissary ahead of them to ready the way. '

In the back seat of the car, Scott cradled his bandaged hand protectively as Tom continued to speak. 'A dark spirit called the Ankou forced its way through the gate at Avebury. Its rotting soul now possesses one of the Brothers of Albion.'

'Daedalus?' Scott spat the name in anger.

The old woman's head shook in reply.

'No, the Dead Lords found someone much more useful to their plans: General Charles Buchanan, a top officer in the British Army. The Ankou is manipulating him to ready the country for the Dead Lords return. On the midsummer solstice, when the borders between the worlds are stretched to their thinnest, the Dead Lords will channel their power to the Ankou, helping it to summon an army of the dead.'

The cramped interior of the car fell silent; the incessant patter of rain drumming against the roof the only sound as they struggled to take in Tom's words.

'What can we do then, Dad?'

Avalon's voice broke through the silence, heavy with hopelessness.

'Whilst the Dead Lords are trapped in limbo, the Ankou's power is limited. You need to find this weapon you're searching for and use it to destroy the Ankou before it's too late. If you don't, it will bring back the dead in an endless army. All of them. Everyone who has ever lived.'

The old woman's breathing was growing shallower, every breath squeezed through her teeth in a strained hiss.

'Find General Buchanan. Stop this fiend inside him.'

The woman's body shuddered. Scott saw the pupils focus for a moment, before rolling back beneath her eyelids. When her lips trembled open again, the low rumble of Tom's voice sounded as if it were fading into the distance.

'I can't stay in this poor woman's body any longer.'

Her body shook again, the car seat juddering as she reached out with a trembling arm and took Avalon's hand in her own.

'I'm so proud of you.' Tom's voice was a faint echo. 'Remember I'll always be with you now.'

Avalon's shoulders shook as her fingers tightened around the old woman's. Then the woman's hand suddenly jerked away, her body twisting in the driver's seat as it spasmed uncontrollably. Her arms shot forward, hands locking around the steering wheel as Avalon looked on helplessly.

'Dad!'

The word escaped from Avalon's lips in a half-sob, but the only answer that came in reply was a guttural, gargling sound that emanated from deep inside the old woman's throat before dwindling to a sigh.

The old woman opened her eyes, blinking owlishly as she focused on the line of cars ahead. The traffic was slowly starting to move again as a yellow-jacketed roadworker waved them forward past the cones. She turned towards Jason, her face creased into a puzzled frown as he eyed her warily.

'I'm – I'm going to have to drop you off at the next services,' she said, her stuttering voice restored to its feminine softness. She reached down towards the gearstick with a trembling hand. 'I really need to stop and have a cup of tea.'

She put the car into gear, rolling it slowly forwards past the line of roadworks, the hulking JCB diggers silent as the workers huddled out of the rain in their prefabricated huts. From the back seat, Scott saw the woman glance back in the rear-view mirror. As he caught her gaze, she quickly looked away but not before he'd seen the glimmer of fear lurking behind her eyes.

Deep down, she knows, he thought; *some primal instinct is warning her to get away from danger as quickly as she can*. In the seat next to him, Avalon sobbed silently into her scarf. A road sign reading BRISTOL 43 MILES flashed by as the Fiesta picked up speed. If an army of the dead was coming, then they had to find the weapon that could fight against them. They had to get to Tregillian Vau.

CHAPTER TEN

'Gentleman, I appreciate the candour with which you have spoken today. As the new Minister for Defence, it is vital that I have a full understanding of the dangers that our country faces, both from conventional threats and the more recent terrorist attacks that have plagued our roads and motorways. Rest assured that the government will give you all the resources you require to protect our proud nation and ensure that Great Britain remains a secure haven in an increasingly uncertain world.'

Jerry Daedalus clasped his hands together as he brought the meeting to a close. Around the long table, the air marshals, admirals, generals and assorted civil servants murmured their assent. Rising to their feet, the military top brass took their leave of the minister, slowly filing out through the meeting room doors. The gold braid on their uniforms glittered in the summer sunlight which shone through the high windows of the Ministry of Defence. As the last of the officers turned to leave, Daedalus held out his hand to halt him.

'General Buchanan, if I could just detain you for a moment. There's a minor matter that I wish to discuss with you.'

One of the minister's civil servants hovered by the door, his eyebrow raised questioningly to check if his presence was required.

'I won't be needing you for this, William,' Daedalus said with a dismissive wave of his hand. 'This is a private matter.'

With a respectful nod the civil servant withdrew from the room, closing the doors behind him to leave the two men alone.

General Buchanan stared at Daedalus, the soldier's craggy features set in an unreadable expression.

'What is it you want to discuss?'

'Our plans to open the Dead Ways are at risk from an unexpected quarter,' Daedalus replied. 'A loose end that should have been tied up when we unlocked the First Gate at Avebury now needs attending to. Jason Dyer, Scott Williams and the girl Avalon Moody have learned of a weapon that can be used against anyone who tries to open the Dead Ways again. They are on their way to Tregillian Vau in Cornwall to find it.'

A shadow passed across Buchanan's face.

'We need to stop them,' Daedalus continued, 'The new golden age that will dawn on Albion's shores when the Dead Ways are opened cannot be endangered by their interference.'

The minister turned towards the wall, a map of the British Isles framed above the meeting room table. He gestured towards the far south-west corner, the long toe of Cornwall poking into the Atlantic Ocean.

'The local police down there are incompetent halfwits, not to be trusted with such an important undertaking. This mission requires military intelligence. I want you to take a detachment of troops to Tregillian Vau. Find the weapon and destroy it for good.'

The general's coal-black gaze glittered with malice.

'And the children and their policeman protector?'

'Eliminate them,' Daedalus replied.

CHAPTER ELEVEN

The rain started to fall once more as they tramped down the narrow lane, the fading sunshine that had welcomed them to Cornwall just a distant memory as evening turned to dusk. High skeletal hedgerows rose up on either side of them, gnarled masses of knotted branches with thorns that plucked at their clothes as they passed. Avalon led the way, peering down at the rain-spattered map, the twilight quickening as they trudged through the puddles in search of the fogou at Tregillian Vau.

Scott set his face against the rain, craning his neck as he tried to peer over the hedge line. They had arrived late that afternoon in Tregillian, a tiny village buried at the very edge of the Cornish peninsula. The lorry driver who had dropped them off had shaken his head as they stepped down from his cab.

'Backside of beyond here,' he'd told them before gunning his engine and heading on for the town of Penzance.

The village was a single road lined with stone-built houses, bound at one end by a grim-looking inn whilst at the other, a squat church tower lay half-hidden behind castellated gates. Whilst Scott and Avalon had skulked outside, Jason braved the local shop, asking the grizzled shopkeeper for directions to the Tregillian Vau fogou. The shopkeeper had eyed Jason suspiciously, his three-day old stubble now merging into the beginnings of a beard, but eventually the man had grudgingly sketched out a rough map and directions on the back of a local guide book he'd forced Jason to buy. Before he left, Jason had glanced nervously at the newspaper on the counter and saw that the report of the police hunt for the three of them had been pushed off the front page by the headline GOVERNMENT CONSIDERS MARTIAL LAW TO STOP MOTORWAY TERROR ATTACKS. The date emblazoned on the top of the newspaper reminded him how little time they had left. June 18th. Three days until the midsummer solstice when the Ankou would unleash a merciless army of the dead.

Turning right at the store, they'd headed down a narrow lane, quickly leaving the village behind as Avalon traced their route on the hastily drawn map. 'The fogou's at the farm,' the shopkeeper had told Jason, the words rolling from his tongue in a thick, phlegm-tinged accent. 'Highfield Farm up towards the lighthouse at the Watch.'

Now, as the lane sloped down towards the coast, the squat white tower of the lighthouse was silhouetted against the grey curve of the Atlantic Ocean stretching out beyond the headland. The sea merged seamlessly with the sky as thick sheets of rain gathered strength.

From behind the hedgerow, a mournful lowing was answered in turn by a deep bellow. Then, around the next bend in the lane, the hedgerows finally parted to reveal a ramshackle wooden gate with a roughly painted sign reading HIGHFIELD FARM – PRIVATE PROPERTY. Behind the gate, a muddy track led up to a low stone-built farmhouse, its chimneys jutting from each corner of the roof. In the farmyard outside, a herd of Friesian cows were clustered around a water trough in the lee of an old stone wall.

'OK,' said Jason as he wearily pushed the gate open. 'Let's find out if this journey's been worth making.'

His shoes squelched through cloying mud as the three of them dodged past foul-smelling puddles. The farmhouse sat in darkness and as they reached the unlit porch, Jason could see the paint peeling from the weather-beaten wood. The glass in the windowpane above the door was cracked and the entire house seemed blighted by an air of decay.

Jason rapped his knuckles against the door. The loud knocking echoed across the farmyard, causing the cows to moo nervously as they shied away from the disturbance. Jason waited. No answer. He turned back towards Scott and Avalon, both of them ankle deep in the oozing slurry.

'There's nobody here.' He glanced around the gloom of the farmyard, the cows almost invisible in the fading light. 'I don't know if we're going to be able to find the fogou tonight – not without any help.'

'We've got to try,' said Scott, his voice firm against the biting wind that swept off the sea. 'We're running out of time.'

The three of them fanned out across the farmyard. Scott trudged past the shadows of the farmhouse, heading towards the cattle sheds at the far side of the yard. The creeping darkness was almost impenetrable now, broken only by the blinding beam of the lighthouse beacon that suddenly swept across the farmyard, illuminating the scene for a second in a brilliant glare, before disappearing out across the sea.

As he tramped through what he hoped was mud, Scott could almost taste the stench of slurry that stuck to the back of his throat. His feet sunk into the slime as he neared the cattle sheds; the agitated lowing of the cows growing louder as he approached. A biting wind swept in from the sea and Scott shivered, not from the chill, but from the raw ache of the wound on his palm. He glanced down at the bandage wrapped around his right hand, the white material stained crimson again. Why wouldn't it heal? He could feel the freezing pain pulsing through his veins, and if he closed his eyes, he could seem monstrous forms of the Dead Lords clawing at the sky above the Avebury stones.

'Over here!'

Avalon's voice rang out. Turning, Scott could see her silhouetted against a low stone wall, the cows lowing nervously as they edged away from her presence. Trudging back through the sickly stench of the mud, Scott reached

Avalon at the same time as Jason, the two of them arriving to see her leaning over a pitch-black opening at the base of the wall.

'I think I've found it,' she said, her eyes flashing with excitement through the gloom. 'This is the fogou.'

Close up, Scott realised that what he'd thought was an old stone wall was actually a low earthen bank faced with rough slabs of stone packed tightly together. The entrance to the fogou was hidden halfway down the bank, a small square window of blackness peering down into the earth. Squatting down in the mud, the wound on his hand throbbed as he stared into the abyss. Their last hope – a weapon that could strike down the Dead Lords. Could it really be hidden in this scruffy hole in the middle of a stinking farmyard?

A flickering glimmer of light illuminated the stones around the entrance of the fogou as Jason shielded the flame of his lighter against the rain. Just beyond these, Scott could see slabs of stone lining a narrow passageway that dropped steeply into the darkness.

'What are we waiting for?' he said.

Scott clambered forward, slipping through the narrow entrance and stepping down into the dark interior of the fogou. The earth was wet and sticky beneath his feet. He rested his hand against the flat slabs of stone lining the passage walls, the rock cool to the touch. The walls curved upwards to create a low ceiling that caused Scott to stoop as he turned to gaze up into Avalon and Jason's faces as they clustered around the hole.

'Are you coming?' he asked them.

The faint light from the entrance was momentarily eclipsed as first Avalon then Jason clambered down into the subterranean slipperiness. Waiting in the darkness, Scott could feel the blood pumping through his veins; the throbbing pain from the wound on his hand a constant reminder of why they were here.

The walls were suddenly illuminated with a sickly yellow glow as Jason flicked his lighter on. He held the flame in front of him, his shoulders hunched as his head grazed the slabs of ceiling stone. Scott looked around the small circle of light. The rough stone walls were covered in a creeping green lichen as the long low passage stretched back into the darkness.

He felt a tug at his arm and turned to see Avalon's face emerging from the shadows, her eyes widening in wonder.

'I know it's here,' Avalon breathed, her hushed words echoing through the fogou. 'I can feel it.'

Scott slowly nodded. He could feel it too – a strange electricity hanging in the stillness of the air; the silence broken only by the dripping sound of water beading on the stones.

'Let's go and find it.'

With Jason leading the way, his lighter throwing out a flickering pool of light, they descended into the depths of the fogou. The passageway narrowed as they edged forward,

Scott stumbling over the fallen stones that lay half-buried in the slippery floor.

Ahead of them, a quartz stone embedded in the wall shone with an eerie light. The tunnel veered left here, running forward for a few more steps before ending suddenly in a tumble of stones. No way past. In the unearthly glow Scott glimpsed an opening at the base of the wall, a small square of blackness, maybe eighteen inches high.

'Look.'

Tugging on Jason's arm, Scott directed the lighter downwards, its flame sucking greedily at the stagnant air. A tiny stone-framed entrance, so low only a child could think of crawling through it, hinted at the further depths of the fogou. As Jason held the lighter steady, Scott squatted down, squinting into the darkness to see a low clay-cut passageway glistening with moisture.

'This must be the creep passage,' whispered Avalon, her voice still unnaturally loud in the confines of the tunnel. 'It should lead to the chamber at the heart of the fogou.' She crouched down next to Scott, the shadows dancing across her face. 'That must be where the weapon is hidden.'

Jason shook his head. 'There's no way on earth I can get through there,' he said as he eyed the hobbit-sized hole.

Even Avalon looked less enthusiastic now that she could see the thick mud carpeting the cocoon-like tunnel as it stretched down into the darkness – an oozing stickiness warding off anyone thinking of entering.

'I'll go.' Scott said. He held up his hand for the lighter, the flame jumping as Jason reluctantly handed it over. Scott slid down onto his belly, ignoring the water that instantly started seeping through his clothes, and peered into the pitch-black fissure. 'I don't think more than one of us could get down there anyway.'

'Scott.' Jason's voice echoed behind him as Scott edged himself forward, slithering inside the narrow opening. 'Be careful.'

A damp stickiness surrounded him as he pushed his way forward, his elbows sinking into the mud. The flickering flame of the lighter was warm against his face, illuminating the narrow tunnel carved out of the earth as it sloped downwards. He couldn't turn now or even look back over his shoulder, only drag himself forward on his stomach, every movement taking him deeper into the heart of the fogou. Scott could feel a strange rhythm pulsing through his body as he slithered through the tunnel, an ancient energy thrumming through the earth.

The damp air crackled with electricity before the flame from the lighter suddenly guttered and died, plunging Scott into the absolute darkness of the grave. Panicking, he flicked desperately at the wheel of the lighter, but heard only the answering hiss of spent gas.

The darkness licked at Scott's face. He only had one thought – to escape from this prison. He tried to push himself backwards, but the tunnel seemed to tighten around him and his hands slipped in the mud, slapping his face down into the sticky darkness.

As he lay there choking in the rotting earth, there was a faint flash of light ahead of him in the tunnel. Scott scrambled forwards, his hands scrabbling for purchase in the damp clay as he desperately sought the sanctuary of the light. The earth surrounding him was getting colder and wetter with every frantic movement he made as he half-slithered, half-swam through the freezing slime. Another flash illuminated the tunnel as he felt the earth around him shake, a sound like gunfire rumbling through the fogou.

Scott looked up in confusion and was almost blinded by another volley of flashes, freezing the scene in a sequence of strobing images.

Ahead of him, he could see another figure crawling through the tunnel, worn leather boots kicking their way through the mud.

Another explosion of light flooded the tunnel, the force of it sending Scott sprawling as a blastwave of sound washed over him.

When he lifted his head again, he could see the figure still crawling doggedly forward.

'Wait,' Scott called out, his voice almost lost in the aftershock.

As he squirmed forward, sliding through the slime in pursuit, Scott saw the tunnel start to widen. He caught a glimpse of the crawling man's mud-splattered clothes, a khaki uniform – a soldier's kit maybe – its brass buttons shining dimly in the afterglow. Gaining ground, he was only inches behind the man as another volley of flashes ripped through the tunnel.

Scott reached out with a flailing hand, grabbing hold of the man's ankle.

'Who are you?' Scott demanded. 'What are you doing here?'

He tightened his grasp, trying to haul the man backwards as he dragged himself up alongside. As well as the mud encrusting the archaic uniform, Scott saw with a shudder, deep scarlet bloodstains soaking through the side of the man's weather-worn tunic. The soldier turned towards him revealing a face twisted in a snarl of burnt flesh and bone. One eye, caked in blood and dirt, blinked as it slowly focused on Scott; the rest of the man's face was blasted away in a grotesque mask of rotting flesh.

'Is that you Tommy?' The soldier's words escaped in tiny bubbles of blood from his ripped open jaw.

Scott recoiled in fear, burying his face in the mud to escape the horror of the man's questioning gaze. Stagnant mud, heavy with the scent of rotting corpses, filled his nostrils. Choking, spluttering he pulled his face free from the slime.

The soldier was gone; the darkness of the tunnel closing in around him once more.

There was no choice. No way back. Only forwards.

Scott could feel jagged rasps of breath at his back, but he screwed his eyes shut as he scrambled forwards, slithering downwards into the depths of the fogou.

He didn't know how long he'd been crawling for. Every second in the darkness felt like an age. Dragging himself deeper, the earth beneath his fingers became colder, drier, older even. The thought of the prize hidden at the heart of the fogou drove him on.

Gradually, Scott realised that the low roof of the tunnel was no longer pressing down on his back. He reached out in the darkness, his hands groping in vain for walls that were no longer there. He dragged himself up onto his knees, his body slick with slime.

He had escaped from the tunnel, but as he peered into a darkness as black as the end of time, Scott couldn't tell where his journey had brought him.

'Hello.'

Hello. Hello. Hello. Hello. Hello.

His voice seemed to echo without end.

'Is there anybody there?'

As his words rippled out into the void, Scott strained to hear any answering reply. He could sense a presence out there in the blackness, but could hear nothing as he listened intently.

Scott stepped forward, the ground beneath his feet a cold, hard stone. This must be the place he had seen in the picture. The cave at the end of the world. The weapon that could defeat the Dead Lords was somewhere in this darkness.

He took a second step forward, the echo of his tread reverberating through the chamber in an endless flurry of footfalls. As he took another step his foot slipped, sending him sprawling on the freezing stone. The impact knocked the breath from his bones. As he lay there, he could feel the darkness pressing in on him, pushing him back, reluctant to give up its secrets.

'Please,' Scott begged in a cracked whisper. 'I need your help.'

The darkness swallowed his words and buried them in silence.

Then Scott saw a faint glimmer amidst the blackness. A tiny speck of light that grew steadily larger and brighter until its incandescence filled the vast cavern. In the very heart of it was the figure of a woman.

Scott shaded his eyes, the intensity of the light burning his retinas.

Ghostly flowing robes that shimmered with an unearthly glow floated through the stillness of the cave. The woman looked down at Scott through glittering eyes, her face stern, severe, beautiful. Skin as pale as alabaster shone as though lit from within.

WHAT DO YOU WANT?

The words appeared instantaneously in Scott's mind.

'You've got to help us,' Scott pleaded. 'They're going to open the Dead Ways. Three days until the summer solstice and then they'll unleash an army of the dead.'

His words rushed out in a babble of sound.

Scott looked up and met the pale lady's gaze. Her eyes glinted like a diamonds, a pitiless stare that dried the words on his lips as his voice finally trailed into silence.

IF MAN DECIDES TO OPEN THE DEAD WAYS, THEN I CANNOT STOP HIM.

'But they think they are going to open the gates to some promised land. They don't realise the truth.' Scott shook his head in dismay. 'The Dead Lords are using them – manipulating them to carry out their plans before they destroy us all. Please,' he begged. 'The book said you had a weapon – something that could stop them.'

The woman stared into Scott's eyes, her gaze a piercing brilliance that seemed to peer inside his soul. She held out her hand. A shimmering iridescent light glowed in the heart of her palm.

YES.

Scott was spellbound, his eyes drawn inexorably to the globe of light taking form there.

ALBION'S LAST HOPE.

Her words echoed in Scott's mind.

ONLY USE THIS GIFT ONCE. AT THE THRESHOLD BETWEEN THIS WORLD AND THE NEXT.

Without thinking, Scott reached up with his wounded

hand, fingers caked in mud and slime, the bandage lost somewhere in the depths of the tunnel. He could feel the heat radiating from the light, like the warmth of the sun on a perfect summer's day.

The pale lady gazed down at him, the fierce beauty of her face sculpted in sorrow.

'Thank you,' Scott breathed as he closed his bloodied fingers around the shimmering globe.

The moment his hand closed around the light Scott was plunged into darkness.

'Wait,' he called out as sticky blackness began to tighten around him again. 'Where do we go? How do we stop them?'

The walls of the tunnel were collapsing. The sodden earth filled Scott's open mouth, burying his shout in silence. Out of the darkness, her words came rumbling through the earth.

FIND THE GRAVES. WHERE THE GIANTS DANCE AT THE SERPENT'S TEMPLE. FIND THE GRAVES.

He was dragged back into the blackness. The void rushing around him before the tunnel finally vomited him out onto a cold, rocky floor.

Scott felt hands reaching out, lifting him to his feet as the spark of a match lit the scene with a flickering glow.

'Are you OK?'

Jason was leaning over him, his face creased with concern. Behind him was Avalon, the flame of the match cupped in her shaking hands.

'Did you find it?' she asked, her voice trembling with excitement.

Scott looked down at his mud-soaked clothing; black streaks of slime covered every inch of his body, the stench of rotting earth filling the air. His right hand was still clenched tightly shut. He could feel a silken fragility in the heart of his palm.

'Yes.'

Scott opened his hand to reveal the weapon the pale lady had given him. Albion's last hope.

The bud of a white rose, its furled petals curled tightly around itself, nestled in the hollow of his palm.

'That's it?' Jason couldn't hide the scorn in his voice. 'We're going to stop the Dead Lords with a flower?'

Scott scowled in reply as Avalon dropped the dying match to the ground, darkness momentarily rushing in to claim the fogou again before she struck another match into life. Under the flickering flame, Avalon peered closely at the rose, its curling petals tinged with amber.

'Look at your hand,' she said, her voice shaking with disbelief.

For the first time, Scott noticed the skin beneath the flower. Where the flesh of his palm had been torn apart, not so much as a scar remained. When Avalon had helped Scott change the bandage earlier that day, his hand had still been disfigured by the festering wound. Now the skin was unblemished, his hand restored.

'What happened in there?' Avalon asked.

'I saw her,' Scott replied as he carefully slipped the ivory bud into his jacket pocket, safe from harm. 'She told me what we need to do – where we need to go.'

He turned to lead them back out of the darkness, a charcoal square of sky just visible in the blackness ahead.

'We need to find where the giants dance at the serpent's temple,' he told them. 'We need to find the graves.'

'What's that supposed to mean?' Jason asked impatiently. 'What graves?'

'I don't know,' Scott admitted, shivering in his soaked-though clothes. He clambered up, squeezing his way out of the fogou's narrow entrance. The farmyard was shrouded in darkness, the night sky completely devoid of stars as storm winds blew in across the sea. Reaching back, he helped Avalon and then Jason as they scrambled clear. The blackness around them was almost as dense as that in the fogou. Even the cows had disappeared into the darkness. 'The pale lady told me that we only have one chance to stop them – at the threshold between this world and the next.'

A sudden blinding beam of light caused Scott to shield his eyes in surprise. This wasn't the lighthouse beacon sweeping across the farmyard, but an unwavering torch beam pointing directly at him.

Scott froze in fear. His first thought that the Brothers of Albion had found them, that Daedalus himself was at the other end of the torch beam.

Then, the light was slowly lowered and a figure stepped forward out of the darkness. Scott saw a stout man dressed in a greasy green jacket, a checked cap pulled low over a crown of snowy-white hair. A pair of piercing eyes fixed Scott with a questioning stare, the weather-beaten face creased into a craggy frown.

'So you've seen her then.'

CHAPTER TWELVE

Scott cupped his hands around the steaming mug of tea, the warmth slowly spreading through his fingers. The farmer banged the kettle back down on the range and turned to the table where the three of them sat waiting.

The bulb in the broken lampshade overhead filled the kitchen with a pale yellow light. Outside, Scott could hear the howl of the wind, rattling the windowpanes as the tatty floral pattern of the curtains shivered in the breeze.

'Are those clothes alright?' the farmer asked gruffly as he sat himself at the head of the table.

Scott nodded. He fingered the collar of the checked shirt he was now wearing. It was a couple of sizes too big and smelt of mothballs.

'Perfect. Thanks.'

The farmer shook his head dismissively.

'It's no trouble. Those are my son's old clothes. He left them here when he went off to university. Said he'd be back to help me run the farm when he got his degree. He's working as an accountant now over in Plymouth.' He took a slurp from his mug. 'So are you going to tell me what you were doing down that fuggy hole?'

'Look,' said Jason casting a warning glance towards Scott and Avalon. 'We're grateful to you for taking us in, but it's like I said, we got lost, we were looking for shelter from the storm when –'

'You know what's down there,' Scott interrupted, his fingers picking at the wound that was no longer there. 'You said it yourself, you've seen her haven't you? The lady at the end of the world.'

The farmer fixed Scott with an unblinking stare.

'Aye,' he said finally. 'I've seen her. Just like my father and his father before him. This farm's been in my family for centuries, but she has always been there. Watching over the farm, watching over the world.' He took another gulp of tea, his hand shaking slightly as it brought the mug to his lips. 'But this past year, her gaze has been turned away.'

'What do you mean?' asked Scott, the image of the pale lady's glittering eyes still burnt into his brain.

'These are bad times,' the farmer said flatly. 'Bad times.'

The lines on his face wrinkled into deeper furrows as he began to explain.

'Each cow on this farm used to produce nearly three hundred gallons of milk a week but, for these past six months, every time I've tried to milk the herd all that has come out of their udders has been stinking pus and blood. At spring, during calving season, I had to watch the local vet pull deformed and lifeless calves from their mother's wombs. Not one survived. Not one.' The farmer shook his head with a shudder. 'They looked more like monsters than any calves I'd ever seen.'

Scott's flesh crawled at the thought.

'And worse than that,' the farmer continued. 'Two months ago, my dog Jess got sick and died. I buried her out on the back field where it overlooks the sea. Then last week, I heard the cows panicking in the field. When I went out there, I saw a dog chasing them down, harrying the older ones in the herd and attacking them. I thought it was a stray at first, but then I saw Jess's empty grave and I realised it was her. Back from the dead. The bones were sticking through her fur where the flesh had rotted away.'

The farmer's hands trembled as he stared into the distance, reliving the memory.

'I called out to try and stop her. Fired a warning shot, but she just turned and came straight for me. Sixteen years I'd had that dog – since she was a pup. But when she ran across that field towards me, there was blood in her eyes. I had to shoot seven times before she stopped.'

The farmer fell silent for a moment as the hideous image festered in their minds.

'That was the last time I saw the pale lady. I took what was left of Jess down into that fuggy hole. Asked her what was happening – why she had abandoned us.'

Scott saw the old man's eyes glistening with tears.

'She said the land was dying, the natural order of things slowly unravelling, and there was nothing she could do.'

The farmer looked up to meet Scott's stare, the lines of his face drawn in a worn mask of worry.

'But you know all this don't you? She said that someone was coming. Someone who was trying to hold the darkness at bay. She told me that I should help you.' He glanced around the table at Jason, Avalon and Scott. 'I didn't think you'd be so young. Can you really stop this chaos?'

Scott held the old man's teary gaze. He could feel the shape of the tiny rosebud still hidden in his pocket; hear the pale lady's commands still echoing in his mind.

'Yes,' he nodded, his voice low but determined. 'But first I need to find the graves.'

'The graves?' The farmer frowned, the creases in his brow deepening into crevasses.

'That's what the pale lady told me,' Scott replied. 'Find the graves – where the giants dance at the serpent's temple – find the graves.' He looked up into the farmer's puzzled eyes. 'Do you know what she means?'

The old man shook his head.

'No I don't,' he said, fixing Scott with a pleading stare. 'But if the pale lady told you that then you have to find them fast. Please, for all of our sakes.'

They had left Tregillian Farm early that morning, the farmer pressing the keys for his Land Rover into Jason's hand.

'Take it,' he'd told them, his weathered face creased into an attempt at a reassuring smile. 'You can bring it back when you've saved the world.' Two days left until the solstice. Jason had driven them eastwards along the winding Cornish roads, the cryptic words that Scott had heard in the depths of the fogou the only clues they had to guide their route. *Find the graves. Where the giants dance at the serpent's temple. Find the graves.*

Sitting in the back of the 4x4, Avalon tapped at Dylan's mobile, the battery icon in the top corner of the screen showing its last bar. Her finger slid down the screen as she scanned the internet search she'd brought up, hunting for any mention of the serpent's temple.

'Have you found anything yet?' Scott asked, turning back in the passenger seat as the Land Rover came to a T-junction at the end of a narrow track, Jason peering past the high hedgerows to check the way was clear.

Avalon shook her head.

'There's a Serpent's Mound up in Scotland, a Serpent's Well in Oxfordshire, even a Dragon Hill, but no mention of a serpent's temple. Are you sure that's what she said?'

'I know it was,' Scott replied, every word the pale lady had spoken burned into his mind. His hand reached up to his pocket and traced the shape of the fragile rosebud still hidden there. Albion's last hope. But they didn't even know where to go – driving round in circles, scrabbling to unlock riddles. They were running out of time. '"Find the graves", she said. Where did she mean?'

'She could have meant anywhere,' said Avalon, rubbing her eyes in frustration as she scrolled down the screen. 'There are thousands of ancient graves scattered across the country. Long barrows, burial mounds, passage tombs and cairns. The landscape is littered with the bones of the dead.'

Scott shivered even as a faint shaft of sunlight broke through the clouds. He remembered Tom's words, uttered from the old woman's pinched red lips.

'Your dad said they were summoning an army of the dead,' he said. 'An endless horde to purge the country, ready for the Dead Lords return. Do you know what he meant?'

Avalon looked up through dark frightened eyes, the colour draining from her pale face.

'Everyone who has ever lived rising again from the grave to serve the Dead Lords,' she replied, her words half-whispered in fear. 'An immortal army of the dead, resurrected to slaughter the living. They'd be unstoppable. We'd be outnumbered, overwhelmed – there are so many more of them than there are of us.'

Scott struggled to take in the scale of what Avalon was saying. forty-eight hours until the midsummer solstice. And then an army of the dead would be marching down every road in Britain. 'How many?'

Avalon shook her head.

'There are more than sixty million people living in Britain right now, but think about all those lives stretching back in time; hundreds and thousands of years. There must be billions of the dead. We wouldn't stand a chance.'

Scott and Avalon slumped into silence, the only sound the muddy growl of the Land Rover as Jason changed gear.

'We don't need to find this serpent's temple to stop this army of the dead,' Jason said, glancing in his rear view mirror as they neared another junction. 'We just need to find General Buchanan. He's the one that's been possessed by this evil spirit – the Ankou.'

'That's right.' Avalon seized on Jason's words. 'If we find the Ankou, we can stop the army.'

'But how do we find General Buchanan?' Scott asked.

'I already have,' Jason replied, glancing towards Scott with a sly smile. 'At the farmhouse last night whilst you were sleeping, I did a little digging. It's difficult to find the location of soldiers on active duty, but there's always ways around this if you know the right questions to ask.'

Scott stared at Jason, unable to believe that he'd kept this hidden from them.

'Why didn't you tell us?'

Jason flicked up the indicator as he pulled the Land Rover onto the slip road, pressing down on the accelerator as he sped to join the rushing line of traffic heading east on the A30.

'I'm telling you now. I didn't want to speak in front of the farmer,' he replied. 'General Buchanan is currently posted at Larkhill Barracks in Salisbury. Apparently he's taken charge of the training of a company of elite troops there – all very hush-hush.'

Scott's heart sank. The image of an army camp protected by high barbed-wire fences and soldiers with guns standing guard filled his mind. Would they have to take on the British Army just to get to General Buchanan in the first place?

'What's the plan?' he asked. 'How are we going to get to Buchanan?'

'We get to Larkhill Barracks,' Jason replied. He swung the 4x4 past a dawdling caravan, overtaking it as the road ahead cleared. Above them the morning sun was breaking through the scattered clouds, the first real warmth they'd felt for days. 'Then we'll find a way.'

CHAPTER THIRTEEN

The farmer sat hunched over at his kitchen table, his hands wrestling with each other as he watched the soldiers ransacking his farm. The contents of the kitchen drawers and cupboards were emptied on the floor around him: broken plates, knives and forks, candlesticks and tins of food. The fridge door hung open, spilt milk spreading from a smashed jug that lay on the stone-tiled floor. From upstairs in the house came the sound of breaking glass, the heavy tramp of soldiers' boots stamping across the ceiling.

Two soldiers dressed in camouflaged combat uniforms stood stationed by the door, their rifles held ready for action, whilst standing over the farmer was the figure of their commanding officer. The crowns and stars on his shoulder revealed the officer's rank – but General Buchanan's gaze was hidden behind a pair of sunglasses.

'You've got no right coming in here like this,' the farmer complained, 'Treating me like I'm the bleeding enemy. I served my country too, you know. Was posted to Northern Ireland with the Parachute Regiment before I came back to take over the farm.'

'Be quiet,' Buchanan growled. 'You've harboured known terrorists here. Now tell me where they are.'

The farmer stared up at the general, his weather-beaten face set in an implacable expression.

'I don't know what you're talking about,' he replied with a defiant gleam in his pale-grey eyes.

With a snarl, General Buchanan turned to address his soldiers.

'Wait for me outside,' he ordered.

'Sir!'

Shouldering their rifles, the soldiers trooped out of the door, slamming it shut behind them. For a moment, the farmhouse was still, only the anxious lowing of the cows outside breaking the silence.

Buchanan turned back to face the farmer, resting his palms on the kitchen table as he leaned forward menacingly.

'You better follow them and get off my land,' the farmer grunted, shifting uneasily in his chair. 'I'm not telling you anything.'

'Oh, but you will,' Buchanan hissed. He reached up to remove his sunglasses. In his face, where his eyes should have been, two glittering black orbs stared inhumanly out. As the farmer shrank back in fear, Buchanan reached forward and grabbed hold of his shoulders. 'You must.'

Malevolent beams shot out from the general's eyes, the dark energy invading the farmer's body as it poured itself into his open mouth, his nostrils, his ears and his eyes. Tentacles of black light gripped the old man's face as the Ankou stared into his soul. Trapped in its clutches, the farmer's body shook uncontrollably, a black tide of darkness engulfing his mind. The Ankou could see everything the farmer had seen: Scott, Avalon and Jason emerging from the depths of the fogou; the three of them sat around this kitchen table, Scott telling him what the pale lady had said.

Releasing their grip, the black tentacles slithered back into the depths of General Buchanan's skull. The farmer slumped forward, his head hitting the table with a thud, the glassy gaze of his pale-grey eyes staring sightlessly at the ruin of his home. Reaching down to the table, Buchanan placed his sunglasses back over his eyes.

'Where the giants dance at the serpent's temple,' he repeated softly.

Turning away from the farmer's lifeless body, General Buchanan strode to the door. Flinging it open, he emerged into the sunlight, his soldiers standing to attention as he crossed the farmyard. With a wave of his arm he gestured towards the low earthen bank faced with rough slabs of stone. At its base, the shadowy entrance to the fogou could just be glimpsed, half-hidden in the shade of a water-trough.

'Time for some target practice,' he ordered. 'I want you to blast those stones to smithereens.'

'Sir!'

The soldiers aimed their assault rifles, their sights trained on the low stone wall.

'Now!'

Opening fire, the soldiers emptied their ammunition in a deafening hail of bullets. The bank exploded in an eruption of dirt and shards of stone, the entrance to the fogou obliterated in an avalanche of rubble.

Satisfied with the destruction, Buchanan turned away, striding back towards the jeep parked at the entrance to the farm. One of the soldiers with three stripes on the sleeve of his combat jacket glanced across at the general's retreating figure.

'What about the farmer, sir?' he called out.

Buchanan glanced back, his eyes glittering darkly behind his sunglasses.

'Leave him,' he said. 'He told me what I needed to know.'

CHAPTER FOURTEEN

Smoke curled out from underneath the Land Rover's bonnet, the engine hissing angrily as a grey-milky film of leaking oil pooled on the tarmac beneath their feet. The blazing sun was riding high in the sky, the afternoon slowly creeping by whilst they were stuck on the hard shoulder of the A30, watching the traffic roar past.

Scott turned to Jason who was wiping his oil-smeared hands on a dirty towel he'd found in the boot of the car.

'Can you fix it?'

Jason shook his head.

'The head gasket's blown,' he replied with a grimace. 'We'd have to get it to a garage, get a new part and strip the engine down to replace it. It would take hours. There's no way we'd be on the move again until tomorrow at the earliest.'

Sitting on the grassy bank at the roadside's edge, Avalon looked up from the phone, her eyes darting impatiently from Jason to Scott.

'We don't have hours,' she reminded them. 'The solstice is

the day after tomorrow. We've got to find General Buchanan before it's too late to stop him.'

As Avalon spoke, a police car sped by in the outside lane, its blue and red lights flashing as the cars ahead of it pulled across into the nearside lane. The three of them tensed until the wail of the siren slowly faded away, the police car disappearing into the distance. It wasn't looking for them.

Scott nodded. Avalon was right. Every second they were stood here, the dark spirit of the Dead Lord inside of Buchanan would be working to raise its army of the dead. He ran his hand through his hair, feeling the sweat on his fingers. The words of the pale lady echoed in his mind: *Find the graves – where the giants dance at the serpent's temple – find the graves.*

'Maybe we should forget about Buchanan,' he said. 'Down in the fogou she said that we should find the graves where the giants dance at the serpent's temple.'

'And what does that mean?' Jason replied with an exasperated sigh. 'We don't have a clue. Unless Avalon can find out where this serpent's temple is or a pack of dancing giants turn up to show us the way, we can't waste our time chasing after riddles. We know where Buchanan is and that's where we're going now.'

Biting his lip in frustration, Scott knew that Jason was right.

'Then we've got to get moving again.'

'How?' Jason replied, a flicker of annoyance creeping

into his voice. 'I told you – the engine's shot.'

'Same way we got down here in the first place,' Scott replied, his gaze steeled against the sun. 'We hitchhike.'

They had been walking for nearly an hour, tramping through the undergrowth at the edge of the roadside as the sun beat relentlessly down. Scott led the way, his oversized shirt catching on the tangled bramble that overhung the narrow grass verge between the asphalt and the dense green vegetation beyond. Behind him, he could hear Avalon's grumbling commentary as thickets of thistles and nettles scratched at her ankles, whilst Jason silently brought up the rear.

To their right, a stream of traffic tore past, the thunder of the road almost deafening now that they were free from the confines of the Land Rover. Coaches, cars, lorries and caravans, all streaming past – every single one of them ignoring their outstretched thumbs.

Scott wiped the sweat from his eyes; the hope that had first fuelled him when they'd left the broken-down 4x4 behind was fading fast as the afternoon wore on. In all the time they'd been walking nobody had even slowed down to offer them the hope of a lift. Even on a bright summer's day, every single driver that passed seemed to be wary of the newspaper stories about the horrors that lurked on the roads.

'Police.'

Jason's voice rang out in warning, the three of them quickly ducking back into the cover of the trees lining the embankment. The dense curtain of leaves shielded them from view as, on the other side of the central reservation, a police patrol van sped past.

Scott waited in the shadows, faint curls of sunlight breaking through the leaves and dancing across his skin. Despite the warmth of the day, Scott shivered. Even now as they headed for Larkhill Barracks, the weapon that could stop the Dead Lords hidden safely in his pocket, they still jumped at the sound of every siren, fearful that the Brothers of Albion were around every corner.

'Scott.' He heard Jason's voice calling out from beyond the shade. 'Come on – the coast is clear.'

As he emerged into the sunlight, Jason and Avalon were standing there waiting. For the moment, the road was free of traffic and as Avalon turned to Scott, her dark fringe of hair sticking to her pale face, she shook her head in defeat.

'I don't know if I can go much further,' she said. 'My feet are killing me.'

Glancing up, Scott stared ahead into the distance, his eyes squinting against the sun, as the road began to curve northwards.

'Just a little bit further,' he urged. 'We're bound to reach a service station soon and then we'll have our pick of lifts.'

Avalon slowly nodded her head as the three of them set off again. Cars continued to speed by, the occasional mocking beep of a horn the only acknowledgement of their outstretched thumbs.

As they trudged along the curve of the embankment, the road slowly opened up again and Scott saw a long lay-by set back from the dual carriageway a couple of hundred metres ahead. A convoy of half a dozen dilapidated coaches, buses and camper vans were pulled into the lay-by, their engines idling as, at the top of the banked grassy verge, a ragged row of long-haired men in tie-dyed T-shirts stood with their backs to the road, relieving themselves in the bushes. One by one, the men tucked themselves in, and turned to head back to their vehicles.

Scott set off at a galloping run. The leading coach at the front of the convoy lurched into gear, its right-side indicator flashing as it signalled to rejoin the carriageway.

'Scott!' Jason's shout rang out above the traffic noise. 'Where are you going?'

Scott glanced back over his shoulder as he ran.

'I'm getting us a lift,' he shouted in reply. 'Come on!'

He could see the convoy of vehicles starting to pull out. An old single-decker bus with a rainbow painted on its side slipped out into the nearside lane behind a beaten-up camper van. Sweat slicked from Scott's body as his feet pelted along the narrow verge, desperate to reach the convoy before it was too late. Only one vehicle was still left at the head of the lay-by, a lime-green coach, its exhaust pipe spitting out a smog of fumes as it waited for a gap in the traffic.

Scott's heart thudded in his chest as he drew alongside the coach, his feet slamming against the tarmac as its wheels edged their way forward. The coach began to nose its way out onto the hard shoulder, eager to be on the move. With a last despairing lunge, Scott banged on the coach door causing the driver to slam hard on the brakes.

The door swung open with a pneumatic swoosh as a middle-aged woman, her eyes hidden by sunglasses and her hennaed hair tucked behind her ears, stared down at Scott from the driver's seat.

'I thought everyone was back on board,' she called out. She scratched her head as Scott stood there in his sweat-soaked shirt, panting as he fought to catch his breath. 'Whose bus are you supposed to be on?'

Scott shook his head. He glanced back to see Jason and Avalon stumbling down the grassy verge of the embankment towards the coach.

'Well, what do you want?'

Scott's answer came in a gasp

'We – we – we've broken down. Could you give us a lift?'

The woman pushed her sunglasses up onto her head, scrutinising Scott as Avalon and Jason's sweating figures hurried across the tarmac to appear by his side.

'Where are you heading?' she asked.

'Salisbury,' Jason replied, his arm hooked over Avalon's shoulder as she leaned on him for support.

The woman raised an eyebrow. She hesitated for a

moment, tilting her head to one side as though sizing them up.

'You're in luck,' she replied, gesturing with her thumb for them to climb on board. 'That's the way we're heading too.'

'You're going to Salisbury?' Scott asked as he clambered up the steps to the coach, scarcely able to believe their luck.

'Close enough,' the woman replied as Scott and Avalon climbed on behind Scott. She pressed a button on the dashboard and the doors swung shut with a sigh. Checking her side mirror, she pushed her foot down on the accelerator and the coach swung out onto the A30. 'We're heading to Stonehenge for the solstice.'

CHAPTER FIFTEEN

Scott shaded his eyes as he stared out of the coach window, the late afternoon sunlight slanting in through the glass. He watched the road signs flash by, the M5 now only three miles away as the coach pulled alongside the single-decker bus, both vehicles exchanging blasts on their horns. Soon the convoy would turn north-west, heading for Salisbury Plain and the ancient monument of Stonehenge.

Two seats ahead of him, Jason sat dozing, his head resting on his bunched-up jacket wedged against the window. Next to Scott, Avalon was flicking through the pages of a science fiction magazine that she'd found stuffed in the pocket of the seat in front. The rest of the coach was cosy with travellers: friendly faces, tie-dyed clothes, nose-rings and dreadlocks. Near the back of the bus, a balding man with a grey-grizzled beard picked out a melody on his battered guitar, whilst next to him a smiling baby, held in her mother's arms, clapped happily along. All ages from the young to the old, travelling in one direction and they'd welcomed Scott and his friends on board without question.

Scott shifted uncomfortably in his seat, picking at the fraying fibres of its worn armrest. He almost felt safe. He looked up again as another road sign swept by: one mile now to the start of the M5. If they kept this speed up, they could be in Salisbury by nightfall. Then they'd have twenty four hours to find General Buchanan and stop him from raising an army of the dead.

At the front of the coach, a young man with crusty bleached-blond dreads had taken over the driving. Fraggle, the others had called him. Now their voices rose up in friendly protest as he switched the CD on the stereo and the laidback reggae that had been playing was replaced with a hard-edged techno rhythm.

'It's driving music,' Fraggle shouted back with a grin as the coach accelerated towards the motorway slip road.

Rising from her seat directly behind Fraggle, Scott saw Rose, the woman who had let them on board, start down the aisle towards them. Her long crimson hair fell messily around her shoulders and her suntanned face was lit by a friendly smile as she sat down in the seat across the aisle from Scott and Avalon.

'Are you two OK?' she asked. 'Sorry about the music – Fraggle reckoned he wouldn't make it to Stonehenge without some techno to keep him going.'

From behind her fringe of black hair, Avalon smiled shyly back.

'I like it,' she replied.

Rose tapped her hands against the headrest in front of her

'Me too,' she grinned. 'So, why are you all heading to Salisbury?'

Scott's hand stole silently towards Avalon, his fingers resting on her arm in warning. No matter how welcome Rose and her fellow travellers had made them feel, they couldn't risk their secret with anyone. The eyes of the Brothers of Albion could be anywhere. Even here.

Scott nodded his head towards Jason, the detective's eyes still closed, his mouth half-open as a thin trail of drool hung from his unshaven chin.

'Our dad's taking us to see our uncle – he's in the army,' Scott improvised, his mind fixing on the one thing he knew about Salisbury. 'He's training in the barracks there before he's posted overseas.'

The smile on Rose's face disappeared, a sudden frown creasing her forehead.

'Men with guns,' she said, a bitter tone staining her words. 'Sending more children to kill and be killed.'

She glanced across at Scott with troubled eyes.

'I hope you're not stupid enough to consider joining up?'

Scott shook his head.

'No chance,' he replied. 'I'm not old enough anyway.'

Rose drew her knees up to her chest, clutching her arms protectively around the paisley folds of her long skirt. For a moment, an uncomfortable silence hung in the air between them. Some private pain seemed to be gnawing away inside her.

'How about you lot?' Scott asked, quickly trying to change the subject. 'All these coaches and buses – there must be nearly a hundred of you heading to Stonehenge. What's the big deal?'

Rose looked up, a watery smile slowly creeping back across her face.

'It's the first summer solstice since they closed that blasted road,' she replied. 'No more fences, no more traffic. I don't agree with much this government's done, but they've done the right thing here.'

A slow shiver of understanding crept up Scott's spine. Of course, the A303 was gone now, the road slowly being returned to nature. Another step forward for the Greening of the Roads; another break in the cage keeping the Dead Lords at bay.

'We'll finally see Stonehenge as it was always meant to be,' Rose continued, the rays of sunshine slanting through the window bathing her face in a golden glow. 'This year, we'll celebrate the solstice like the ancients did.'

* * *

The narrow road was rammed with traffic, exhaust fumes filling the evening air as the coach sat idling, the convoy backed up through the tiny village's main street. Daylight was slowly fading and, from the clusters of stone cottages lining the street, curious locals emerged from their homes to inspect the strange vehicles that were disturbing the peace of their rural idyll.

Ever since they'd turned off the motorway to head east on the A39 towards Stonehenge, they'd been snarled up in constant tailbacks. It seemed like every single vehicle leaving the motorway was heading in the same direction, all cutting through the lush countryside in search of the stones. In the driver's seat, Fraggle had been leaning permanently on the horn, alternating honks of greeting to other coach-loads of travellers with angry blasts to urge other road users to get out of their way.

'Getting down to the stones never used to be this bad when the A303 was open,' the bald, bearded hippie called out as he picked out mournful blues chords on his guitar.

At the front of the coach, standing next to Fraggle, Rose glanced back towards Roger, the guitarist, with a glower. Her mobile phone was pressed to her ear and, as she turned away again to face the road, her eyes scanned the horizon searching for a way through the bottleneck of traffic choking the route ahead. The day was slowly giving way to dusk, the long shadows cast by the squat Norman church on the right-hand side of the road creeping towards the coach. The clock on the church's grey stone tower read a quarter to nine.

A small gap opened up in the queue ahead of them. Fraggle pushed the coach into gear with a sigh, pressing down on the accelerator as he edged the coach forward before stamping on the brake again. They had travelled less than ten metres. He looked up at Rose.

'There's no way we'll get there by sundown tonight.'

'I'm on it,' Rose replied, momentarily cupping her hand over the mouthpiece of her phone and then turning away again to speak to the person on the other end of the line.

In their seats four rows back, Scott, Avalon and Jason exchanged worried glances. Their entire plan hinged on reaching Salisbury tonight. They had to get to the army barracks and find General Buchanan before the solstice – before it was too late.

'That's great,' Rose was speaking on her mobile phone, 'we'll be there in half an hour.'

She snapped her phone closed with a smile.

'Change of plan,' she announced to the bus. 'We're stopping off tonight in Glastonbury. Jim's got an old mate there who runs Summerland Meadows Community Farm – the fields run right beneath the Tor. We can camp out there, charge up our energies on the ley line and then set off for Stonehenge first thing in the morning. The worst of this traffic should've cleared by then.'

Loud cheers rang through the coach, the travellers' voices raised in relief at the thought of finally escaping from this endless gridlock. Rose walked down the aisle to where Scott and Avalon were sat, Jason turning in his seat to face her.

'I'm sorry we can't get you to Salisbury tonight,' she told them. 'You're welcome to stay with us and we'll drop you off on our way tomorrow. We've got a couple of spare tents.'

'Don't worry, it's fine,' Jason replied. 'If you could just drop us at the station in the town, we'll make our way on from there.'

'I feel like I'm letting you down,' said Rose. Her dark-green eyes darting back to gaze through the windscreen at the queuing lines of traffic, the distant thump of drums rumbling from the bass speakers of the car in front. 'I didn't realise that the traffic would be so heavy – all these people heading down for the solstice. It's going to be epic. The music, the crowds, everyone coming together to watch the sun rise over the Giant's Dance.'

Rose's final words made Scott's heart leap in his chest. *Giant's Dance.* From the depths of the fogou, he heard the echo of the pale lady's voice.

. . . THE GIANT'S DANCE AT THE SERPENT'S TEMPLE. FIND THE GRAVES.

'What's the Giant's Dance?'

The question burst out of Scott, his voice suddenly loud in the confines of the coach. Rose met his earnest gaze, her forehead furrowing in a puzzled frown.

'Sorry, it's an old joke from when we used to go raving at the stones,' she said. 'Chorea Gigantum – the Giant's Dance. It's what the Romans called Stonehenge.'

Scott's heart quickened. The puzzle they'd tried to unlock, the place they had been told to find – they had been heading towards it all this time.

'You should come,' Rose continued. 'It's an unforgettable experience.'

Scott quickly glanced across at Avalon, seeing the same flicker of understanding flash in her eyes. He looked back up at Rose and slowly nodded his head.

'I think we will.'

CHAPTER SIXTEEN

Scott huddled down on the groundsheet, pulling his jacket tightly around him as the warmth quickly faded from the day. Next to him, Avalon had a book she'd borrowed from Rose open in front of her, a torch held in her right hand as she scrutinised the pages. Dusk was gathering around them. They could hear the soft beat of reggae drifting across the fields, the door to the coach left open as the beam of its headlights illuminated the scene.

The travellers were erecting their tents; a rainbow of flame-retardant nylon sprouting across the field. Scott watched as flysheets were hauled over tent poles and the pegs hammered into the earth. Jason was twenty feet away, frowning as he struggled to slide the aluminium tent pole into the sleeve of an ancient-looking flysheet. Fraggle stood over him, the younger man offering pointers as Jason tried to force the pole into the corner tent pin and shaking his dreadlocks with a smirk as the pole snapped out of position yet again.

Ahead of them they could see the soft green hill of the

Tor, the sun slowly setting to the right of the ancient tower that crowned its summit.

Scott turned to Avalon.

'So it's Stonehenge,' he said. 'That's where we're meant to go. But what about the rest of her message? I thought Stonehenge was just a circle of stones – there's no grave there is there?'

'Stonehenge is more than just the stones,' Avalon replied. She looked up from the book, the reflection of the setting sun lighting tiny fires in her dark eyes. 'It's a ritual landscape stretching across the Salisbury Plain. There are more than sixty tombs, long barrows and burial mounds scattered around Stonehenge.' She pointed down at the book, the yellow glow of the torch illuminating a map showing the landscape around the ancient monument. 'The Great Cursus Barrows, Rollestone Clump, the King Barrows Ridge, Winterbourne Stoke – these are the graves.' Avalon's mouth tightened as she scowled in frustration. 'I don't know why I didn't see it before.'

A dark shadow fell across the book. They glanced up to see Rose standing above them. Her red hair was haloed by a soft orange glow, the last rays of light from the setting sun now creeping behind the Tor. Steam was curling up from the mugs she held in each hand.

'Mind if I join you?' she asked.

Scott shook his head, shuffling along to create space on the groundsheet. Rose handed Scott and Avalon the mugs of steaming cocoa and sat down beside them, tucking her long skirt more tightly over her legs to keep out the evening chill. They sat in silence for a moment, each of them looking out towards the Tor. The dark green hill topped by the squat tower was slowly slipping into shadow, the pink and orange skies fading to a darken blue. Small groups of people, their figures almost indistinguishable in the fading light, were descending the path leading down from the Tor, their steps seeming to quicken as the oncoming night followed them down.

Rose bent her head towards them, a warm, contented smile creasing her face.

'Beautiful, isn't it?'

Scott nodded, but as darkness fell across the Arcadian scene he couldn't stop the prickle of fear that crept up his spine. Only one day left now until the midsummer solstice. Soon an army of the dead would be marching down that hill and across Britain; a slaughtering swarm, drenching the country in blood.

He looked out across the field. Most of the tents were finished now and a cluster of travellers sat around a hastily-built fire. Roger, his bald head now protected under a woollen hat, sat strumming his guitar along to an old Bob Marley song. Jason and Fraggle were still fixing the flysheet to Jason's tent, the detective pegging the guy ropes into position.

Rose followed Scott's gaze.

'He's not your dad, is he?'

Her softly spoken words froze the blood in Scott's veins. He felt Avalon's hand reach for his arm, her fingernails pressing into his skin as he slowly turned to face Rose.

'I don't know what you mean.'

Rose looked at him, shadows falling across her kind face as the night drew in.

'I recognise your face from the papers,' she replied. 'You're Scott Williams, aren't you? The boy who went missing last Christmas after his dad was killed.' Her eyes darted back towards Jason, still pegging down his tent unaware that their cover was unravelling with every sentence that Rose spoke. 'And that's the policeman who everyone says abducted you – and this must be Avalon Moody. His other victim.'

Scott couldn't speak. It felt as though his heart had crawled up into his throat where it was now thudding dizzily, strangling his every thought into a blur of noise. They had to get out of here. He scrambled to his feet, his hand reaching out towards Avalon to take her with him.

Rose's hand reached out for his arm.

'Don't worry, sit down.' Her voice remained calm as her fingers closed around Scott's sleeve. 'I'm not going to say anything. I've been around long enough not to believe everything I read in the papers.'

Scott looked down at Rose, her features set in a reassuring smile. His shadow fell across her face, but he couldn't see a trace of darkness there. Scott shook his head. Things were moving too fast, there wasn't any time left to worry about being caught. He slowly sank back down onto the groundsheet between Avalon and Rose.

'What are you going to do?' he asked.

Rose shook her head.

'I'm not going to do anything. You look old enough to look after yourself and I've given you both plenty of opportunity to get away from him if you wanted to. There must be a reason why you're on the run.'

Scott breathed out a loud sigh of relief.

'But I saw that interview with your mum on the TV,' Rose continued. 'Pleading for you to come back, begging for any sign that you were still alive. She couldn't stop herself crying – she was in a real state.'

Scott's face burned with shame. He remembered the torn page of newsprint, his mother's tearstained face soaked through by the rain. All this time, he'd tried to block out the pain that she must be feeling, her suffering a small price to pay for keeping her safe from the Brothers of Albion. But the barriers he'd built around his heart were crumbling as Rose's words hit home. He missed her so deeply, just like he missed his dad. At least he might see his mum one day, when this was all over . . .

Rose rested her hand on Scott's shoulder as he tried to blink back his tears.

'I'm sorry,' she said softly. 'It's just that I know what it's like to lose a son.'

The three of them sat in silence looking out towards the horizon. On the hill above them, the medieval tower stood in darkness, waiting for the moon to rise. Across the field, Jason had finally completed the construction of his tent and was shaking Fraggle's hand in thanks for his assistance. As Jason turned and started to walk towards them, Rose got up to her feet, her fingers squeezing Scott's shoulder in a parting gesture.

'Think about what I've said,' Rose said as she turned to leave. 'Remember, after tomorrow it'll be Midsummer's Day. We'll celebrate the past and look to the future. New beginnings – a time to make things right.'

Scott looked down at the lights of the town below, a scattering of street lamps and dimly-lit windows spreading out past the darkened fields. He could see the black outline of the coach parked in the field beneath him and the handful of tents clustered around it. They would all still be sleeping, unaware that he'd crept up here alone to find the space to think. He leaned against the wall of the tower, feeling the cold stone press against his back, holding him up when all he wanted to do was run.

Up here on the Tor, where darkness was all around, the pale beam of his torch was nothing more than a pinprick in the vast blackness that hung down from the sky. Scott stepped underneath the arch and peered up through the roofless tower into the darkness beyond, a faint constellation of stars the only light shining through as the moon huddled behind the clouds.

In his left hand he could feel the shape of Dylan's mobile phone. His thumb hovered over the touch-screen. Scott shivered, thoughts crowding his mind – all Jason's words of warning, Avalon's attempts to reassure him – but the only person he wanted to speak to now was a hundred miles away.

He shook his head. In just over twenty-four hours, the midsummer sun would be rising and he would be facing an army of the dead. This might be the last chance he had to speak to her. With freezing fingers, he fumbled the number into the phone and pressed it against his ear. The buzz of the ringing tone sounded unnaturally loud in the quiet tower. The phone rang once, twice, three times. Scott was just about to jab his thumb against the screen to end the call when a breathless voice came through on the other end of the line.

'Hello, who's there? Scott, is that you?'

Scott's heart thudded in his chest; the sound of his mum's voice so close after all this time.

'Yes,' he replied, the word half catching in his throat. 'It's me.'

The phone went quiet. For a moment the low crackle of static was the only sound that Scott could hear. Then a sob broke the silence.

'I thought you were dead!'

His mum's voice spilled down the line in a howl of relief, the words almost lost amongst the tears.

'Mum, don't cry.' Scott tried to find the words that would stem their flow. 'It's OK. I'm OK.'

'Where are you?' she said, her voice still wracked by sobs. 'Why haven't you come home?'

'Mum, you've got to listen to me,' Scott replied, his voice small and alone beneath the darkness of the sky. 'You need to get out of the country. Go back to the States. It's not safe for you here. It's not safe for anyone.'

'What are you talking about?' she said. 'I'm not going anywhere without you. Scott, you've got to come home.'

'I can't come home,' said Scott, tears now rolling down his own face, 'not before I stop them.'

'Stop who?'

Scott heard a harsh click on the other end of the line, an unnatural sound that suddenly filled him with fear.

'Scott, are you still there?'

The realisation hit him. The Brothers of Albion were tracking her calls. Even now, satellites spinning in the darkness above him would be pinpointing his location.

'Mum, I've got to go.'

'No, you've got to come home.' The shapes of the words wrenched themselves out of her tears.

'I love you,' he said.

'Scott, no!'

Scott pressed his thumb against the screen, cutting the

phone into silence. Leaning against the wall, he slowly slumped to the ground, the stone cold and hard beneath his body. He looked out into the darkness, the phone still in his shaking hand. On the horizon he could see faint shades of scarlet beginning to stain the edges of the sky, the dawn of a new day fast approaching.

In his mind he could still hear the click on the other end of the phone line, the harsh sound a testimony to his mistake. What had he done? Scott buried his head in his hands and let his tears overtake him.

CHAPTER SEVENTEEN

Jerry Daedalus looked out across Salisbury Plain, the politician's expensively tailored suit strangely incongruous amongst the khaki and camouflage of the soldiers assembled below him. He could see more than a dozen armoured vehicles and tanks rumbling across the chalk downland, thick whorls of smoke swirling around their tyre tracks as the thud of incoming mortars reverberated across the plain.

Behind the armoured vehicles, a second wave of troops were crawling across the quagmire left behind by the tanks as they advanced on the enemy position, an abandoned red-brick building, its walls crumbling and peppered with blast holes. One soldier broke into a galloping run, a fusillade of gunfire covering him as he hurled a grenade through the building's shattered window. There was a split second of silence, then the thunder-crack of the explosion roared across the countryside. The sun was slowly rising red over the horizon, the scattering sunlight staining the sky the colour of blood.

Daedalus turned to the soldier standing next to him,

the noise of battle muted behind the command bunker's soundproofed glass.

'Are your men ready?' he asked him.

General Buchanan nodded, the rays of the rising sun reflected in his sunglasses.

'Yes,' he replied. 'They're ready.'

'I hope it doesn't come to this,' said Daedalus, a rare flicker of doubt creasing his forehead. 'It's not going to look very good if my first act as Minister for Defence is to introduce martial law.'

'The population deserves to be protected,' General Buchanan replied, a steely edge behind his words. 'My soldiers will give them that protection.'

Daedalus nodded.

'You're right,' he said. 'Since the dawning of the Halycon Days the number of incidents has been increasing: the M23 emergency, the Watling Street event, the Piccadilly Line fire. People are starting to ask questions, they're losing faith in the Greening of the Roads project. Such events are only to be expected of course, as the order of life and death is rebalanced, but the situation needs to be controlled.'

He stared out through the window at the soldiers taking aim from their trenches, their gun barrels half hidden by the smoke rolling across the downs.

'If it gets any worse, we'll have to bring in restrictions on movement, funnel essential journeys onto guarded roads. We just need to guide the population safely through the next six months until the Last Gate can be unlocked. Once the Dead Ways are opened, they'll thank us for the care and protection the Brothers of Albion have provided and we'll finally lead them into the promised land. Into eternal life.'

The minister grimaced as a nearby explosion rocked the command bunker. He shielded his eyes from the sudden glare of the incendiary shell on the plain below them.

'You wouldn't think this was just an exercise,' Daedalus muttered, his hands trembling as he straightened his tie.

'My troops treat every battle as if it were the last,' General Buchanan replied. His cragged face was impassive as he observed the havoc unfolding across the landscape.

Daedalus rubbed his eyes, the politician's face suddenly weary as though sickened by the sight of the fighting.

'How do you think history will judge us?' he asked, 'The last generation on this island to live in fear of death. Do you think they'll understand the sacrifices we have made? Will they think it was worth all the pain?'

Behind his mirrored sunglasses General Buchanan's eyes glittered blackly.

'It's always worth the pain,' he replied.

Daedalus frowned. He opened his mouth, but before he could speak, he was interrupted by the shrill ring of his mobile phone. Turning away from Buchanan, he pulled his phone from his jacket pocket and pressed it to his ear.

'What is it?'

Daedalus's tone was impatient, but as he listened to the

voice on the other end of the line a slow smile started to creep across his lips.

'All of them – are you sure?'

He listened intently, nodding in satisfaction at the reply he was given.

'No, just keep them under surveillance,' he instructed. 'This operation needs a firm hand. I'll make the necessary arrangements this end.'

He ended the call and slipped the phone back into the inside pocket of his jacket. As Daedalus turned back to face General Buchanan, all traces of weariness had faded from the minister's face.

'It looks like I'm going to need your men sooner than we thought,' he said. 'That was Detective Chief Inspector Nicholls – Scott Williams has made contact with his mother. Only a two-minute phone call but they managed to trace it. He's travelling with a coach load of new agers heading to Stonehenge for the midsummer solstice. Local police are monitoring from a distance and they've had visual confirmation that he's still with Jason Dyer and the Moody girl.'

Daedalus stared out from the command bunker, looking east across the rolling plains, the haze of battle still hanging heavy as the sun slowly climbed in the sky. The ancient ruins of Stonehenge were less than ten miles distant.

'Stop them and silence them. I want this loose end tying up for good.'

General Buchanan nodded. He ran the tip of his tongue across the underside of his teeth, as if tasting their sharpness.

'With pleasure.'

*　*　*

The coach slowly edged forward as it attempted to navigate the narrow dog-leg turn, the high hedgerows on the nearside scraping against the windows as, in the driver's seat, Fraggle quietly cursed the route they had chosen. The drive from Glastonbury to Stonehenge should only have taken an hour, but with the A303 now closed, they had been forced to follow a winding route across the border between Somerset and Wiltshire, the coach inching through tiny chocolate box villages – West Pennard, Cannards Grave, Leighton, Tytherington and Corsley Heath – the distance to Stonehenge slowly ticking by on the milometer.

Scott sat with his palm resting against his chin, looking out through the glass as another whitewashed stone cottage slipped by the window. The coach accelerated up the leafy lane, shafts of sunlight breaking through the foliage and bathing the rolling fields beyond in a dappled haze. The sun was high in the sky now, the morning slowly fading into memory, but dark shadows still hung beneath Scott's eyes.

They had set off from the Tor earlier that morning, leaving the ancient hill behind, but every second of the phone call he'd made sheltering in the darkness of its tower still burned in Scott's mind. His stuttered words, the muffled sound of his mother's sobs, the tell-tale click on the other end of the line. He hadn't told Jason and Avalon what he'd done – too embarrassed to admit his misjudgement. He just prayed that he'd ended the call in time, before the Brothers of Albion had the chance to trace it.

Scott shook his head to try and clear his mind, fixing his gaze on the road ahead. The route was clear now, all other traffic melting away as the road climbed across the rolling plain, the midday sun above them reaching its zenith in the sky. Another half an hour maybe and they'd be there.

'We're taking a big risk by coming here.'

At the hushed sound of the detective's voice, Scott and Avalon twisted in their seats to face Jason. Keeping his voice low to prevent his words reaching any of the travellers seated on the coach around them, Jason's worried eyes darted from Scott to Avalon and back again.

'Stonehenge. The Giant's Dance. We're putting all our faith in the words of an ageing hippie, but we still don't know exactly what we're looking for. How are we supposed to find the graves when we don't even know where they're hidden? I still think we should have concentrated on finding General Buchanan first.'

Avalon shook her head, her dark fringe swishing above an anxious frown.

'It's not the general we have to worry about – it's the thing inside him.' She gestured at the book lying open on her lap, yet another one that she'd borrowed from the coach's library. Its tattered pages were headed *A Guide to*

165

the Myths and Legends of Britain and Avalon pointed to a small black-and-white illustration of a spectral figure at the top of one page, a skeletal face peering out beneath a peaked hood.

'The Ankou,' she said quietly.

Scott stared down at the picture, the rough ink work of the image burning with a strange, unsettling intensity.

'The Ankou isn't something I knew much about before,' Avalon continued, her voice dropping to a half-whisper. 'It's a legend of a legend, almost forgotten, at the very edges of folklore. The long-lost memory of an ancient evil. The Ankou – the haggard man, the harvester of souls.'

'What does it say?' asked Scott.

'He collects the corpses of the dead and leads them on their journey to the other side. But not just the dead, he takes the souls of the living too. Men, women, children – anyone who crosses the Ankou's path is destined to fall before his power.' Avalon's face grew pale as she read the final words on the page. 'When the Ankou comes, an army of the dead march in his wake.'

Scott's gaze flicked up from the book to Avalon's face, registering the terror behind her eyes. Through the coach window directly behind her, he could see golden fields stretching to the skyline, the crops rifled by the light summer's breeze, but in his mind's eye he could imagine an army of the dead stalking through the fields, cutting down anyone in their path.

'How do we stop him?' he asked, his face pale.

'I don't know,' Avalon replied. 'It says that no living soul can face the Ankou and survive.'

She glanced around the bus at the travellers sitting in clusters all along the aisle. Near the front, a young woman with cropped blonde hair nursed a baby in her arms, whilst across the aisle Roger picked out a soothing lullaby on his guitar. The mood was sunny, a sense of anticipation slowly building as they neared Stonehenge.

Avalon looked back at Scott, her dark eyes searching desperately for reassurance he couldn't give her. If they didn't find the graves before the Ankou found them . . .

Scott glanced out of the window at the flawless blue sky overhead.

'We've got nine hours until sunset,' he replied. 'That's got to be enough time to find the graves. We'll start at the stones and work our way out –'

A sudden flicker of movement at the edge of his gaze snapped Scott's voice into silence. Craning his neck, he peered out through the window, scanning the sky for a glimpse of the blur of motion that had caught his eye.

'What is it?' said Jason.

'I don't know,' Scott replied. 'I thought I saw something. It must have been a bird or . . . no, there it is!'

Scott jabbed his finger skywards towards a small black object hovering several metres above a copse of trees. Jason and Avalon followed Scott's gaze to see what looked like a model helicopter, its black rotor blades spinning around a central drum, as it slowly descended out of sight behind the canopy of leaves running alongside the road.

'What was that?' Scott asked, his face pressed against the glass.

Jason's eyes narrowed; the familiar shape of the spy drone instantly recognisable from his days on the Met.

'Trouble,' he replied.

The coach was climbing towards the crest of a hill, Fraggle grinding through the gears to find the traction needed to make it to the summit. Blue sky filled the windscreen, the landscape beyond shielded from view. The day was perfect, not a cloud in the sky. On the left, a road sign signalled the way down to the crossroads on the other side of the hill – Stonehenge straight ahead, to the right Salisbury and the A360 and to the left the B3086 and a sign for Larkhill Barracks.

As the coach laboured to the top of the hill and finally crested the rise, Fraggle suddenly slammed on the brakes with a panicked shout.

'What the –'

Directly ahead of them, two armoured vehicles were slung sideways across the highway, blocking the road ahead. Two camouflaged soldiers sat manning the machine gun turrets at the front of each vehicle, their weapons pointing straight at the coach. The bus drew to a halt, its tyres throwing up a cloud of dust. In front of the troop carriers, a patrol of armed soldiers, dressed in green and khaki body armour, marched towards the coach. The soldiers' eyes were inscrutable behind coral-coloured sunglasses, but the guns cradled at their hips glinted dully with menace.

Staring out through the windscreen, Scott twisted back towards Jason and Avalon, his face taut with horror.

'They've found us.'

At the front of the coach, Fraggle leaned out of the driver's side window, his dreads rifled by the breeze as he berated the approaching soldiers.

'What the hell do you think you're doing?' he shouted. 'I could have ploughed right into you.'

One of the soldiers, his unsmiling face almost hidden beneath his combat helmet, strode up to Fraggle.

'Look, we're trying to get to Stonehenge,' Fraggle continued, his voice dropping to a more conciliatory tone as he nervously eyed the soldier's low-slung SA80 assault rifle. 'If you could just let us get past then we'll be out of your way'

The soldier's mouth tightened into a thin-lipped smile. He shouldered his SA80 and nodded his head as if to signal the way through.

Fraggle turned back to the rest of the travellers, huddled in frightened clusters all along the coach.

'It's OK,' he told them. 'They're going to let us through.'

Behind him, the soldier swung his assault rifle around and slammed the butt of his weapon against Fraggle's head with sickening force. Fraggle slumped sideways, his arm catching on the steering wheel, blood spurting from the blossoming head wound and soaking the windscreen with crimson tears. The soldiers were fanning out, surrounding the coach, their guns waving wildly as their fists hammered against the glass.

'Get out! All of you! Move it! Now!'

CHAPTER EIGHTEEN

'Get down!' Jason shoved Scott and Avalon down into the aisle as the coach windows shattered around them. Terrified screams filled the air as a salvo of orders were barked though the broken glass.

'Come out with your hands in the air – now!'

At the front of the bus, Roger sprang to his feet defiantly, swinging his guitar above his head like a weapon as he rushed to the coach doors.

'It's the bloody Battle of the Beanfield again,' he yelled, kicking back against the doors as the soldiers tried to storm the coach.

'He's going to get us all killed,' Jason muttered as he crouched by Scott and Avalon's side. 'Stay here.'

Jason started to move forward, heading towards the front of the coach where more of the travellers were trying to fight back against the ambush.

'I'm coming with you,' said Scott, half-rising to his feet, but Jason pushed him back with a shake of his head.

'You've got to keep yourself safe,' he told Scott, as next

to him Avalon ducked underneath another explosion of broken glass. 'Remember what you've got.'

Scott's hand stole up to his pocket to feel the shape of the tiny rosebud still hidden there. Albion's last hope: the only weapon that could defeat the Dead Lords. He sank back down to his knees as Jason's words hit home. Beside him, Avalon breathed heavily as the soldiers rocked the coach.

Jason set off on a crouching run as, from the opposite direction, Rose crawled down the aisle towards them. Blood was smeared across her face and her eyes were filled with despair.

'I can't wake him,' she cried, gesturing back towards Fraggle who was slumped motionless in the driver's seat, blood dripping from his dreadlocks. 'I think they've killed him.'

Seeing Scott and Avalon crouched there amongst the chaos, a faint spark seemed to flicker in Rose's dulled eyes.

'Quick,' she said, crawling forward until she was almost next to them and then pulling to one side a section of the worn carpet that covered the aisle. Beneath the carpet was a rectangular wooden panel, held in place by two small brass rings. 'Help me get this up.'

Scott and Avalon reached down and, twisting the rings, levered up the wooden panel, sliding it to one side to reveal a shallow boarded crawlspace running beneath the coach.

'We put this in when we kept getting busted by the police back in the nineties,' Rose told them. 'They never thought of looking here.' She gestured down into the hiding place. 'Get in.'

'I – I can't,' Avalon stuttered, her face paling at the thought of climbing down into the cramped space.

Outside the coach, there came the sound of rifle fire, ammunition spat at the sky in a volley of warning shots.

Rose shook her head, pushing Avalon down into the crawlspace with a determined shove.

'It's this or them.'

Reluctantly, Avalon slithered forward on her stomach, the height of the crawlspace barely enough for her to raise her head as she slid down into the darkness.

'You too,' said Rose, turning towards Scott. 'Quickly.'

Scott clambered down into the space behind Avalon, his body pressing against the hard wooden boards. He turned his head sideways for a last glimpse of daylight.

'Why are you helping us?' he asked, looking up into Rose's face, her dark eyes glittering with defiance.

'The army took my son,' she said. 'I'm not letting them take you as well.'

Daylight disappeared as Rose slid the panel back into place, the wooden board sealing Scott and Avalon into the darkness with a click. Scott heard the soft slap of the carpet being rolled back into position and the sound of Rose rising to her feet, followed by a thunder of boot-steps stomping down the coach.

'Why are you doing this?' The muffled sound of shouting

penetrated the cramped darkness of the crawlspace, Rose's voice raised in protest. 'We're peaceful people – we only want to get to Stonehenge.'

The sharp crack of a violent blow was followed almost instantly by an anguished wail of pain.

'Get her out of here with the rest of them.'

Above his head, Scott heard the sound of Rose being dragged away, her low moans quickly fading into silence as the tread of army boots marched her down the aisle. The heavy stomp of a single pair of footsteps came to a halt directly above the wooden panel, the board creaking painfully as the weight of the soldier pressed down on it. Scott felt Avalon's hand reach for his in the darkness, the hushed hiss of her breathing painfully loud in the claustrophobic space.

'That's the last of them, sir.' The voice of a young soldier filtered through the floor. 'The coach is clear – no sign of the children.'

'No matter.' From directly above Scott's head came the sound of a gravelly voice raised in reply. Scott froze, holding his breath to try and keep their presence hidden. 'Subdue the prisoners and take them to the holding point. We'll find the children another way.'

'What about the coach, sir?'

'Take it to the holding point,' the commanding officer replied. 'Then torch it.'

The tread of footsteps slowly marched into silence as the

two soldiers exited the coach. From beneath the floorboards, the sound of the soldier's words rang in Scott's ears. The fragile hope that he had been holding on to, the chance to stop the Dead Lords before the solstice arrived, had been crushed into oblivion beneath the stamp of army boots.

Rose's face smeared with blood. Fraggle's unconscious figure slumped over the wheel. The kindness of the travellers who had helped them rewarded with violence at the hands of General Buchanan's men. In the darkness, despair filled Scott's mind. Jason must have been taken prisoner or maybe even worse . . .

The noise of the engine firing into life sent a rattle through the body of the coach. The stench of fumes began to fill the cramped space, a precursor of the flames to come.

As Avalon pressed her hand to her mouth to muffle the sound of her coughs, Scott pushed hard against the panel directly above his head. The board wouldn't budge. He remembered the brass rings locking it in place. As the coach was pushed into gear and started to roll forwards down the hill, Scott felt himself pitched to one side in the coffin-like space.

They were trapped with no way out.

Scott raised his voice above the thunder of the road as it roared beneath their bodies, the wooden boards of the narrow crawlspace rattling in protest as the coach picked up speed.

'It's no good,' he told Avalon. 'I can't seem to shift it – the panel's locked in place.'

He felt her head knock against his; in the cramped space every bump and pothole was amplified as the stench of petrol filled the scant air around them.

'I can't breathe,' Avalon replied faintly, her voice woozy from the fumes.

Scott couldn't tell how long they'd been travelling for. One minute? Ten? Twenty? Every second inside this cramped prison felt like an eternity. He could taste the acrid burn of petrol at the back of his throat. If they didn't stop soon, they would choke to death before the army could even set fire to the bus.

He thrust his legs downwards, feeling the boards at the very base of the crawlspace pressing back against his feet. Reaching up, he braced himself against the wooden panel inches above his face.

'I'm going to try and let some air in.'

Scott waited as the coach began to slow, drifting around a sweeping bend. Other than the driver, he wasn't sure whether there were any more soldiers were still on board. He had to time this right – not make any premature move that could let them know that the coach was carrying two extra passengers.

As the bus straightened out of the corner, its wheels thudding over yet another pothole, Scott kicked out with all the force he could muster. His right foot crunched against the board and the wood splintered. As the coach changed up through the gears, the roar of its engine drowning out all other sounds, Scott kicked out again. The wooden board peeled away and revealed the tarmac running beneath them, the white lines in the centre of the road flickering past.

A rush of air flooded in through the splintered hole, still tinged with exhaust fumes but more breathable now that their cramped prison had been breached. The thunder of the road beneath them was even louder, but Scott strained his ears, listening for any sound from the coach above that showed that he had been heard. There was nothing.

Twisting his head, Scott could see the outline of Avalon's face in the darkness.

'Are you OK?'

Avalon shook her head, her breath coming in gasps.

'I feel sick,' she replied. 'Those soldiers – they said they're going to burn the coach.'

'Don't worry,' Scott told her. 'We're going to get out of this.'

'It's already too late.' Avalon tried to stifle a cough which turned into a sob. 'General Buchanan got here before us.'

The coach began to slow again, the engine slowly grinding down through the gears until it came to a halt with a hiss of hydraulics. Scott heard the sound of voices from the far side of the bus.

'Any more prisoners on board?'

'No. Just taking this to the holding point.'

'Take it out to the firing range – we could do with some target practice.'

The chilling words were followed by the harsh sound of laughter, then the metallic clang of a gate being opened before the coach moved forward again.

Scott twisted his neck to peer through the splintered hole, trying to get some kind of clue about where the coach was heading, but he could only see the same patch of dusty grey tarmac constantly running beneath the wheels. As the coach stayed in a low gear, travelling no more than 5 miles per hour, Scott could hear the sound of barked orders followed by the synchronised thud of boots marching past.

'Stay quiet,' he whispered in warning as the coach hissed to a halt again. 'Something's happening.'

From above them, the sound of the engine suddenly cut out. For a moment, everything was still, a ringing silence filling his ears after the constant drone of the engine noise. Then he heard footsteps clomping down the aisle, followed by splashing sounds. A sudden whiff of petrol fumes filled the air and Scott felt the liquid slowly begin to drip through the board above his head.

Next to him, he heard Avalon gasp, twisting her body away as she tried to escape the burning touch of the petrol soaking into her clothes. Above them, the sound of footsteps retreated as the coach doors hissed open and heavy boots stepped down onto the tarmac.

'It's done – petrol primed and ready to burn. Just let me get clear.'

As a stinging tear ran down his face, Scott twisted his body, contorting his shoulders in the confined space to try and grasp the splintered end of board and prise it free.

Avalon's fingers found purchase on the wood, but it wasn't enough. 'Scott!'

Her voice hissed in his ear as the sound of army boots retreated across the tarmac. If he couldn't get them out of here in the next thirty seconds, they would be toast.

Scott grabbed hold of the splintered end of the board, his fingers scrabbling for a hold next to Avalon's. They wrenched at the wooden panel, feeling its edge buckling under the strain. The hole was getting bigger. Another pull and they could get themselves through.

'Hurry!'

With a final grunt of exertion, Scott ripped the wood apart, his body jerking backwards as the board clattered onto the tarmac beneath the coach. He twisted his head to meet Avalon's frightened gaze.

'Follow me.'

They slithered forward, their clothes soaked with petrol, as they crawled out through the hole. Twisting his neck, Scott glanced past the wheels in the direction the footsteps had fled. In the middle distance, he could see the figure of a soldier shouldering his assault rifle as he took aim at the coach.

The entire coach was doused in petrol – its fuel tank full and ready to blow. One spark was all that was needed, but the squaddie taking aim fifty metres away was going to unleash a cavalcade of fireworks. Scott grabbed hold of Avalon, dragging her in the opposite direction, their skin scraping against concrete as they scrambled clear of the coach.

Ahead of them, beyond a tangled line of razor wire strung at the edge of the road, was an open field. High stalks of corn shone with gold as they swayed in the summer breeze. Scott tugged at Avalon's arm as the two of them launched themselves forward in a desperate race for the wire. He yelled out, a single syllable stretched to breaking point as the world around them seemed to slow and blur into a freeze-framed moment.

'Run!'

Scott heard a distant popping sound as the rifle fired. Then the whoosh of the explosion tore through the air, picking up their bodies and flinging them forward. Scott watched the ground fall beneath his feet, his fingers torn from Avalon's arm as the scorching blast wave hurtled them over the tangled knots of razor wire. His mind was almost disconnected from the unfolding chaos: the muffled *whump* of the coach exploding in a firestorm of twisted metal and shattering glass. Scott felt almost serene as the golden stalks of corn whipped past his face, the ground rushing up to greet him as he finally blacked out.

'Scott.'

He heard the whisper of his name, the sound of it seeming to come from far away as he slowly opened his eyes. Above him, framed by a golden halo, Scott saw Avalon, her dusty face streaked with tears.

Scott felt a jolt of pain streak down his left side as he pushed himself up from the ground.

'Don't worry – I'm fine.'

He glanced across at Avalon. A fresh bruise was blossoming on her forehead, half-covered by the hair falling across her shaken face. The stench of petrol clung to her clothes and her skinny legs were covered with scratches.

'Are you OK?'

Avalon slowly nodded her head, her dark eyes filling again with tears.

'I don't know how we escaped. One more second and . . .' Her voice tailed into a sob, the terrible thought hanging in the air between them.

Scott reached out, awkwardly draping his arm around Avalon's narrow shoulders as they shook with tears.

'It's OK,' he said, 'we made it.'

Avalon shook her head.

'It's not over.' They were crouched near to the field's edge, hiding behind a golden screen of corn. Avalon leaned forward, parting the stalks with her hands to reveal the scene beyond. 'It's only just starting.'

Twenty metres away, on the other side of the razor

wire, the coach burned. Flames leapt through the shattered windows, curling greedily upwards as they engulfed the front of the bus. Behind the pall of smoke, they could see more soldiers marching across a disused roundabout, yellowing grass trampled beneath their boots. Abandoned roads branched off to the north, south, east and west, the cracked tarmac of the forgotten A303 marked by the tyres of the two armoured troop carriers parked in the shadow of a looming structure on the far side of the junction.

Rising up out of the earth like a sleeping ice giant, a huge long barrow dominated the landscape. The glittering mound rose ten feet high and stretched back hundreds of feet towards the long, low horizon where the sun was slowly starting to dip in the sky. The hard earth was piled high to a peak, layers of chalk encasing the grave so that it shone bleakly against the rolling Salisbury Plain, the barrow as white as the bones it was built to keep. A house of the dead.

Along the top of the monument, piles of soft chalk were heaped at regular intervals, running along the length of the barrow like the humps of a serpent's back.

'The Serpent's Temple,' breathed Scott, the words of the pale lady echoing in his mind.

FIND THE GRAVES. WHERE THE GIANT'S DANCE AT THE SERPENT'S TEMPLE. FIND THE GRAVES.

This was it.

CHAPTER NINETEEN

Jason gagged. He fought hard to take a breath as the heavy canvas hood clung to his face, the drawstring pulled tight around his neck. The foul air he'd already breathed a hundred times was trapped with him inside the darkness. He couldn't see a thing and the only sound he could hear was the muffled tread of heavy boots all around him. The plasticuff ties binding his hands together cut hard against his wrists as a sharp weight slammed into his back, sending him staggering forwards.

The sudden jolt of pain jarred his mind out of its frozen state. His thoughts rushed in on him again in a whirl of confusion – countless questions firing back and forth. Where were they taking them? How had they managed to track them down? What was going to happen next? Somewhere out there, marshalling the ranks of soldiers that had taken them prisoner was General Buchanan and the dark soul of the Ankou that possessed him. Had Scott and Avalon managed to escape from its clutches?

His mind grabbed hold of this last question, reliving

again the brutal sequence of events back at the coach. He tried to make sense of the carnage: the barked volley of orders as the soldiers forced the travellers from the vehicle at gunpoint, clubbing anybody who dared to fight back to the ground. The glimpse of Fraggle's prone body laid out on a stretcher, the slight rise and fall of his chest the only sign of life. He remembered seeing Rose, dragged backwards by her hair down the steps of the bus, blood dripping from a broken lip. He'd tried to intervene, but felt the swift blow of cold steel smash against his face and the rest was darkness.

Jason tried to hold on to the last fragment of hope he had left. He hadn't seen Scott or Avalon taken prisoner. He prayed that somehow they were still safe. It was their only chance.

As he was shoved forward again, the butt of a rifle planted between his shoulder blades, Jason felt the warmth of the sun quickly fade from his back. His shuffling footsteps echoed slightly as the ground slowly sloped beneath his feet. The suffocating air inside the hood was stale and warm, but on his exposed arms he could feel a chill prickle against his skin. They were heading underground. As Jason stumbled over a loose stone, losing his footing as he pitched forward in the darkness, the realisation hit him like a hammer. He was walking into a grave.

He felt rough hands drag him to his feet, pushing him forward again with a sharp command.

'Move!'

Jason scrabbled his way along in the darkness, hauling one foot in front of the other as the uneven ground continued to slope beneath his feet. The hood pressed against his face, the choking taste of his own breath burning in his throat. Suddenly, Jason felt the ground begin to level beneath him, the thunder of boots in front and behind him echoing more loudly now.

'Halt!'

The barked order stopped Jason's footsteps in their tracks. From beneath his hood, he could hear the low murmur of voices and he strained to make out the words.

Get them lined up and into the cages ... Orders are to keep them under guard until the general arrives ... We're dealing with terrorists here ...

The sharp point of a weapon pressed against Jason's back, forcing him forward again. Close by, he heard a man's voice call out in protest followed by the sharp crack of violence and then silence. Trapped in the darkness, Jason desperately tried to keep himself calm. He needed to work out exactly where he was and what was going on here before making any rash moves.

With a brutal shove, he was manhandled into a narrow cramped space, cold stone pressing in from both sides and behind him. There was the sound of a bolt being drawn, then the harsh clang of steel as a metal bar pressed down hard against his chest. Jason gasped inside the suffocating hood. He couldn't move – the bar of the cage keeping him locked in a standing position. He fought to take a breath, the metal bar cutting into his chest as air ebbed from his lungs. From all around, there came the clash of steel against stone, broken only by the sound of muffled sobs.

• • •

Jason didn't know how long he had been standing there. Minutes bled into hours, his senses disorientated – impossible to keep track of time trapped there in the darkness. His knees were bent to try to relieve the pressure of the metal bar bearing down on his chest, but sharp stabs of pain constantly darted up his legs as he leaned back against the stone.

Near to him, he could hear soft moans of pain, tormented whispers smothered into silence. He tried to speak – desperate to find out who was still there with him in the darkness, but his own voice could only croak in a shredded sigh. His head hung heavy on his shoulders. It was useless. He was going to die.

Suddenly, he felt hands around his neck, the drawstring loosened with a sharp tug and the hood was pulled back to reveal a blinding light. Jason blinked, the brightness of the room burning his eyes after so long in the darkness. Through flickering eyelashes, he struggled to take in the scene.

Standing directly in front of him was an armed commando, the choking hood that had been tied around Jason's neck, now limp in the soldier's hand. The soldier was standing in a broad stone chamber, some ten feet high, its circular walls lit by powerful halogen lights fixed to the ceiling slabs. Narrow recesses were built into the walls of the chamber at regular intervals, each one holding the bowed figure of a person, a horizontal steel bar caging the prisoner inside. Jason glimpsed the bloodied faces of Rose, Fraggle, Roger and the other travellers from the coach as they were slowly unmasked by the soldiers.

As the soldier stepped away, Jason saw a long dark passageway facing him from the opposite side of the chamber. Above this entrance, a narrow aperture was made where two stone slabs met, and through this slit he glimpsed a glimmer of sky, a small patch of darkness streaked with violet. Jason shuddered. It was night already and, from the look of it, dawn would soon be on the way.

He rattled the bar impotently. Trapped! And on the eve of the solstice, the night would be mercilessly short.

From the passageway, Jason heard the ominous tread of boots approaching. Then, through the entrance, a tall figure in a dark green braided uniform, the crowns and stars on his epaulettes proclaiming his rank, strode into the chamber. His cragged face slowly emerged from the shadows, his features fixed in a gaunt glacial pallor; his eyes were still hidden behind sunglasses even in this subterranean chamber.

Although the disorientating pain still jarred at his senses, Jason knew who this figure was in an instant. He stared at the man, glimpsing the shadow of his skull beneath his skin.

General Buchanan.

The soldier who had torn the hood from Jason's head quickly stood to attention, shouldering his weapon and greeting General Buchanan with a crisp salute.

'Sir! Prisoners restrained and contained as ordered. Sir!'

Standing in the centre of the burial chamber, Buchanan slowly removed his sunglasses. He stared back at the soldier through cold, malevolent eyes, two pale pinpricks of light surrounded by the blackness of the void. When the general finally spoke, Jason didn't hear the gruff tones of a grizzled army officer, but the harsh guttural rasp of a voice that hadn't been heard for thousands of years – the voice of the Ankou.

'It is time.'

A flicker of doubt crossed the face of the young soldier.

'What do you mean sir?'

In answer, the general strode forward and seized hold of the soldier, his vice-like grip dragging him painfully to his knees.

'Kill them all,' the thing inside of Buchanan growled, pointing at the prisoners with a long pale finger. 'The dawn is approaching and my army needs fresh blood.'

'But sir, you can't mean that,' the soldier protested, his voice squeezed to a croak as the general's fingers closed around his throat. 'Under the Geneva Convention, these prisoners are under our protection.'

The general tightened his grasp, his pale fingers whitening

as the soldier gurgled in pain. The click of bones cracking like tiny gunshots echoed around the chamber as the other soldiers looked on in horror. Loosening his grip, Buchanan let the soldier slump to the stone, his lifeless eyes staring up blankly at the moonlight-coloured slabs of stone that glittered in the ceiling.

'You will be the first,' he hissed. 'The first of my soldiers to march for the stones. As the sun rises over Stonehenge, I will bring forth an army of the dead to scour the land ready for our return.'

Jason watched sickened as Buchanan stepped away from the dead body with a slavering hiss of hunger. All around him, the other soldiers were moving in slow-motion, their minds unable to process the reality of what they'd just seen. A young squaddie nearest to the general raised his rifle with a shaking hand.

'Sir – what are you doing? Get down on the floor with your hands above your head.'

The thing that was Buchanan turned with a growl, swiping the weapon from the soldier's hand with a single blow. The general spread his arms wide, his outstretched limbs silhouetted in the glow of the halogen lights and his voice echoing around the burial chamber.

'Every dead soul rises today.'

From the tips of his fingers, icy-grey tendrils of light slowly curled out and clawed at the air. The blossoming streams of energy filling the chamber with a ghostly glow.

With a flick of his wrist, a tentacle of light shot forward from the general's finger, wrapping itself around the neck of the nearest soldier.

Gasping for breath, the squaddie sank to his knees, his fingers scrabbling at his throat as the icy tentacle tightened its grip. The throbbing light poured itself into his mouth, cutting the soldier's choking scream into silence. He writhed in agony against the stone, the light burning through his skin and revealing the bones underneath. His body twisted, contorting as the blinding light wrapped itself around his bones, his skin crumbling to dust in front of their horrified eyes.

As the soldier's withered body lay discarded on the cold slab of stone, the shifting light took on a new form, rising up from the dust as streams of energy still blossomed from the general's fingers. The ghostly figure of a towering warrior, a cruel grin slashed across his skull-like face, drew his sword in salute to the general, its shape almost transparent in the shifting light. As the rest of the soldiers shrank back in fear, the tentacles of light surged forward again wrapping themselves around the fleeing troops, a noose around the neck of every living man.

Trapped behind the steel bar that caged him, Jason saw an icy finger of light arrowing straight for his head. He recognised the twisting talon from the Avebury stones and knew with a shudder the agony it would bring. Jason struggled to focus on what Buchanan was doing, but all he could see was oblivion racing towards him. As the cold hard light engulfed him, he heard the general's voice bellow in triumph as the ghostly company of the dead rose in the burial chamber.

'We march for the stones.'

The blinding white tide finally overtook Jason and he slumped in the cage, his bleached bones luminous beneath his shrivelling skin.

CHAPTER TWENTY

Scott and Avalon shivered in the shadow of the long barrow. The wind howled across the rolling Salisbury Plain as, less than a mile away, the broken circle of Stonehenge sat half-veiled by the darkness. Scott felt as though they had been crouched there forever, his legs and arms sore from where they had crawled through the mist-shrouded fields to reach this spot. It had taken all their energy and cunning to get as close as this without being spotted.

A short distance away, the north-east face of the burial mound looked out towards the distant stones, its shadowy entrance framed by huge stone slabs cut into the chalk. Half-hidden by the trees that still lined the abandoned road, Scott watched as a dark figure marched inside the long barrow, disappearing into its depths. The ghostly outline of the burial mound was set against the darkness of the night sky, the horizon slowly stained with violet as the dawn approached.

For hours the camouflaged uniforms of the soldiers had been moving like shadows around the perimeter of the long barrow, scurrying backwards and forwards as they secured the site. An advance guard of six soldiers had taken a band of hooded prisoners inside the burial mound when the sun had still been high in the sky. Scott thought that he'd glimpsed Jason amongst them, but he couldn't be sure. Now only a scattered band of soldiers patrolled the abandoned road that skirted the monument, their silhouettes dwarfed by the high banks of exposed chalk. The remaining soldiers waited in silence, standing sentry at the entrance to the mound.

Scott fought to keep the fear at bay, struggling to stop his mind racing in terror from the thought of what was to come. They had come here to prevent the Ankou from raising its army of the dead, but with the travellers trapped inside the burial mound and the ranks of armed soldiers guarding the entrance, they were powerless to stop it. He twisted his neck towards Avalon, his face pressed against the tree trunk as the roar of the wind died away.

'What are they waiting for?' he asked through frozen lips.

Avalon twisted her head to reply, her bobbed black hair whipping across her face as the reflection of the towering burial mound glittered in her frightened eyes.

'They're waiting for the sun to rise.'

Suddenly, as one, the voices of the soldiers rose up in alarm; a confused cry ringing across the desolate landscape. General Buchanan was marching out from the darkness of the barrow, his gaunt glacial features wreathed in shadows.

As he stepped forward, the general was flanked on both sides by shimmering spectral figures, a legion of warriors emerging from the depths of the burial mound. The ghostly shapes of Vikings, Roman legionaries, crusaders and bowmen – an eerie company of the dead.

'Sir – what is this? What are you doing?'

The soldiers barked the questions in disbelief, fumbling for their rifles as the shining figures advanced upon them. The thing that was Buchanan raised its arm high, a cruel grin slashed across its malevolent face.

'Open fire!' he growled.

From behind the general, a volley of ghostly spears and arrows arced through the air, cutting through the ranks of soldiers with a blazing light. As the soldiers fell back with agonised screams, Scott watched in horror as the flesh rotted from their bones where the weapons hit. The stricken soldiers stumbled, the blazing light quickly consuming them from within, as their bodies crumbled to dust and bones.

On the horizon, a blood-red glimmer of light crept across the darkness. The night sky and the landscape started to separate as a new day dawned. His arm outstretched, General Buchanan gestured towards Stonehenge, the ancient stones glinting strangely in the half-light.

'To the stones,' he cried. 'We must call our brothers from their graves.'

Scott felt the air prickle with electricity, an ancient energy pulsing across the plain. With General Buchanan at their helm, the twelve shimmering warriors of the dead began to march across the landscape. Their ghostlike figures skimmed across the chalk downs as they headed towards the heart of the circle.

In the shadow of the long barrow, the small band of soldiers who had been patrolling the abandoned road broke cover. Seeing their comrades fall, the soldiers charged at the spectres, firing hundreds of rounds from their SA80 assault rifles as they advanced. The roar of their weapons was deafening, the ground exploding in a hail of gunfire, but the bullets just cut uselessly through the ghostly figures, their stately procession to the ancient monument unimpeded.

At the rear of the shadowy platoon, the ghost of a grizzled commando, his translucent skin glowing with an unearthly light, turned and raised his own weapon in return. The short stub machine gun spat a sea of living fire across the plain; incandescent streaks of light devouring the pursuing soldiers in a funeral pyre.

Scott felt like everything was happening in slow motion. As he watched the soldiers fall, their skeletons crumbling to dust as the bullets struck, he heard the echo of the pale lady's words. They had found the graves at the Giant's Dance, but now as Avalon crouched beside him in the cover of the trees, the two of them were just silent spectators.

As dawn crept across the sky, Scott saw a thin sliver of sun slowly emerge from the heart of Stonehenge. The halo of sunlight spread towards the ridge of the topmost stone, which lay on top of two huge pillars; a rough-hewn doorway of light bathing the monument in a blood-red glow. At the head of this ghostly procession, Buchanan was less than half a mile away from the stones. He'd be there in minutes.

'We've got to stop them before they reach the stones,' said Scott, twisting towards Avalon.

She glanced back at the looming shadow of the long barrow, the rising sun bathing the vast chalk mound in an ethereal glow. Framed at the base of the tomb, its dark entrance stood open – unguarded.

'Whatever's brought those things to life,' she said. 'It's buried in there. We've got to find it and stop it.'

Scott nodded his head.

'You go,' he told her, his eyes still fixed on the ghostly warriors closing in on the stones. 'I've got to stop Buchanan.'

Scott set off for Stonehenge in a crouching run, Avalon's anguished call after him lost to his ears. Scott's trainers skittered across the broken tarmac, dodging past the cracks and potholes as he ran through the shadows. His heart thudding in his chest, Scott prayed that none of the ghostly figures gliding towards the stones would look back. Buchanan was marching with his arms outstretched, silhouetted by the rising sun. The light stretched across the rolling plain, sweeping past the horseshoe of upright stones and catching Scott in its piercing glare.

Half-blinded, Scott stumbled on the rolling plain. He tumbled forward, then quickly caught himself as he fell, his hands slamming against the earth. Pulling himself back to his feet, Scott's hand stole up to his pocket to feel the shape of the tiny rosebud still hidden there. Albion's last hope. The only weapon that could defeat the Ankou before it raised its army of the dead. He just prayed that he'd get a chance to use it. He looked up again, the grey stones of Stonehenge bathed in a blood-red light as Buchanan led his ghostly company into the heart of the circle.

• • •

Avalon stood at the entrance to the long barrow. Huge slabs of stone were set into the chalk and directly in front of her a dark passageway led down into the depths of the tomb. With a nervous glance back towards the distant stone circle, Avalon stepped through the shadowy entrance. Beneath her feet, the flat slabs of stone slowly sloped away and Avalon could hear the echo of her footsteps, unnaturally loud in the darkness. In her mind, grim imaginings of what waited below began to take shape.

The narrow passageway suddenly opened up, ushering her into a broad stone chamber. The cavern glittered fiercely with the same ethereal glow that took shape in the ghostly figures descending on Stonehenge, and she saw with jolt of fear the corpses held captive in its walls.

Twelve wizened bodies were caged upright behind horizontal steel bars, each imprisoned in one of the narrow recesses that encircled the chamber. Avalon stepped forward, frantically searching for any sign of Jason but found her eyes drawn to the nearest skeletal figure.

Her heart pounded in her mouth as she stared up into a face of withered flesh clinging to the dead man's skull. Cold, lifeless eyes stared back at her blankly, and beneath the wasting skin she saw bones that burned with a phosphorescent fire. Clothes hung from the man's wasting frame and with a sickening lurch, Avalon recognised the shirt that Jason had been wearing. She started to turn away in horror, but glimpsed the soft rise and fall of Jason's chest. He was still alive.

Avalon grabbed hold of the steel bar and tried to wrench it open, but it was locked into place. She struggled uselessly to break the thick padlock securing the bolt to the stone, her pale eyes shining with fear as the strange glow burning through Jason's frame filled the chamber. She had to find a way to free him.

Turning away, Avalon frantically searched for something to break open the prison. On the floor of the chamber, she saw scattered weapons, handguns, rifles and army knives, discarded amongst the dust. Stooping, Avalon snatched up a handgun from the dusty slabs of stone. The handle was still warm; with trembling fingers, she aimed the barrel straight at Jason's chest.

The gun fired in an explosion of noise, the bullet shearing through the thick padlock, sending it falling to floor with a clang. The metal bar fell open and Avalon rushed to catch Jason's withered body before it slumped to the floor.

Across the plain, on the threshold of Stonehenge, General Buchanan turned in confusion. The undead soldier who had been marching by his side slowly melted into the air with a discorporate howl. With a growl of frustration, the thing inside of Buchanan turned back towards the long barrow.

'Onward,' he ordered the spectral warriors. 'They still resist the call of death.'

As the ghostly soldiers started to sweep across the plain, their spirits returning in vengeance to the place that had birthed them, Scott stepped out from the shadows of the stones, his fingers closed tightly around the fragile rosebud in his hand.

Framed in the huge stone doorway, General Buchanan turned towards Scott with a guttural hiss.

In his face where his eyes should have been, two glittering black holes stared inhumanly out. As Scott took a step backwards in shock, he saw the absolute evil of the Ankou lurking in the void of those bleak craters. Behind him, the rays of the rising sun were climbing above the horizon and the lightening sky was stained a deep red.

Buchanan advanced to meet Scott, a snarl consuming the lower half of his face.

'At last . . .'

At the heart of the burial chamber, Avalon cradled Jason's head in her hands, his skull still visible beneath the parchment-like skin. As she watched, Jason's mouth slowly opened, the rotting stumps of his teeth bared in a death rictus. He raised a pale skeletal finger and pointed at the rows of corpses still held prisoner in their cages. His voice came in a cracked whisper.

'Save them.'

Avalon leapt to her feet. The gun still in her hand, she stepped towards the nearest recess, the cadaver held there trapped in its cage. Avalon took aim and fired. The padlock exploded with a furious squeal and the cage's steel bar swung open in reply. As the haggard body slid to the floor, Avalon was already racing to the next cage, repeating the action again and again and again. As each body fell free from its prison, the eerie flickering light that filled the chamber faded until only one prisoner remained.

From the passageway, there came a guttural shriek of fury and the dark shape of the last of the undead soldiers swept into the chamber. The ghostly figure of a Viking warrior stepped forward with a growl as, at his feet, Avalon crouched protectively over Jason's emaciated body. With a flailing arm, the Viking swept Avalon aside. Her frail figure slammed against the stone and slid to the floor like a discarded doll.

With a hand that was almost corporeal, the ghostly warrior seized hold of Jason's throat. Dazed, Avalon pulled herself up into a sitting position, shaking her head to try and clear the fog of pain. Across the chamber, the Viking squeezed his fingers around Jason's windpipe. With the gun still held in her fingers, Avalon took aim with a trembling hand. She only had one chance to get this right.

The gun fired and the padlock holding the last prisoner in place exploded in a shower of sparks. As the body caged there slid to the floor, the ghostly warrior standing over Jason melted away with an anguished howl. Released from his clutches, Jason slumped to the floor as Avalon rushed to his side. His feeble gasps told her that somehow he was still alive. As she held Jason in her arms, Avalon could only hope that Scott was too.

Scott raised his right hand, the rose still hidden in his grasp, but Buchanan seized hold of his fist, his vice-like grip dragging Scott to his knees. Pain contorting his face, Scott tried to break free, but the general was too strong. He dragged Scott inside the broken circle of stones, the ancient monument humming with a strange vibration as a halo of sunlight crowned the ridge of the topmost stone. At the very heart of the monument, a broken block of greenish-grey sandstone lay embedded in the earth.

'This is the altar stone,' Buchanan growled as he slung Scott to the ground, his head cracking against the slab of stone. A cruel grin of triumph was slashed across the general's face as he drew a long army knife from the folds of his uniform, its steel blade glinting in the dawn. 'I shall follow the old ways,' he said. 'Then my army of the dead will march from the stones and this land will be ours again.'

Scott froze in fear, terror pumping through his veins at the sight of the blade. His mind flashed back to Avebury, the memory of the pain coursing through his body. He couldn't live through that again. He only had this chance. Thrusting his hand out in front of Buchanan's face, Scott opened his palm to reveal Albion's last hope.

The white rosebud sat crumpled in the hollow of his hand, a single white petal falling uselessly onto the cold, hard stone.

The thing inside of Buchanan laughed with a sound like the grinding of ancient gears, then he drew the blade across Scott's throat.

CHAPTER TWENTY-ONE

Scott was lost in a world of mist and shadows. Drifting alone in the darkness, he tried to remember how he got here, the fragments of thoughts all jumbled and distorted in his mind. One moment he'd been lying across the altar stone and then Buchanan –

The memory snapped in two. Scott felt himself falling, tumbling towards the glittering banks of the long barrow as the screams of the dying filled his ears. The scene shimmered with an unearthly light, hard earth and stone made almost ethereal in this twilit dream. He could see Stonehenge beneath him: the ghosts of the stones a menacing darkness that sucked the light out of the sky and at the heart of the circle, the black disc of the sun. He felt himself falling towards it, the sun dragging him down into its gaping maw. Waiting for him there was the Ankou – its true form finally revealed.

Scott's mind reeled in horror as he saw the shapeless, mutating creature: a vast floating monstrosity hanging in the void. Hundreds of eyes turned towards Scott's ghostly form and tumorous mouths gaped hungrily as he fell towards the swirling black vortex of flesh. Blubbery tongue-like tentacles reached out, grabbing hold of Scott as he screamed in a whiplash of pain.

The agony was a thousand times worse than at Avebury as the Ankou squeezed its tentacles and Scott's soul twisted in torment. It felt as though he was being consumed, everything that made him human – every emotion, every memory – was slowly stripped away. The vast inky shadow of the creature shivered in delight as it dragged Scott towards the endless row of slavering mouths.

In the darkness, a fragment of thought sparked in Scott's mind. He could feel the shape of it still nestling in his closed fist. Albion's last hope. As the agony overwhelmed him, with his last ounce of resistance, Scott opened his hand.

An iridescent light glowed in the heart of his palm. As Scott watched, the light grew larger and brighter, burning with a blazing intensity as it spilled out from his hand. The light twisted into searching tendrils of white fire that plucked the tongue-like tentacles from his body.

The Ankou quailed as the dazzling light darted towards its monstrous form, its multitude of mouths screaming in terror; wide open in fear. The blazing light burned through the Ankou, the monstrous creature melting with hideous groans. Scott watched as the black vortex of its flesh shrivelled into a cold grey flame that finally fell without a sound into the black hole of the sun and disappeared.

He had destroyed it. The Ankou was gone.

Scott was floating with his arms outstretched, his body silhouetted against the sun's ebony disc. All his pain was gone and he could feel the primal energy of the Dead Ways pulsing through him; the power of life and death at his fingertips. Looking down at the ancient tomb, he saw Jason's body slumped in the burial chamber at the heart of the long barrow, flickering on the border between life and death. Scott shook his head.

'No.'

Reaching out with pale fingers, Scott pointed towards Jason, shards of sunlight stretching out and illuminating his flickering form. The Dead Ways pulsed through his fingers with an ancient power.

In the shadow of the tomb, he saw Jason's chest begin to rise and fall again, the flesh growing back onto his bones as his pale stretched skin glowed with new life. Scott watched as the detective slowly pulled himself to his feet, Avalon staring at him in astonishment.

Then Scott turned his gaze towards the other bodies lying slumped on the floor of the chamber. The people who had helped them, tried to keep them safe. Reaching out again, his hand silhouetted in the sunlight, Scott unfurled his fingers and watched as the figures rose to their feet, hands reaching up to unblemished faces as they gazed down in wonderment at their restored bodies. Rose, Fraggle, Roger, the rest of the travellers from the coach – each and every one of them safe.

The Dead Ways flowed through him. Scott knew he could do anything. With the power at his fingertips, he could stop the Dead Lords once and for all.

'Scott.'

The voice came from behind him, the gentle tone that he thought he would never hear again. His father's voice.

His heart hammering in his chest, Scott turned to see his father standing in the shadow of the sun. He wanted to run to him, to feel his dad's arms around him again, hugging him close, but he was trapped floating in the void between one world and the next.

'I'm so proud of you,' his father said.

Scott wanted to tell him how much he'd missed him, but none of that mattered now as he looked into his dad's pale-blue eyes.

'I can make it all right now. I can bring you back. Tom can come back too.' Scott's words raced out in a torrent of hope. 'I can make everything as it should be.'

His father looked back at Scott, his face creasing in sorrow as the shadow of the sun lengthened around him. He shook his head.

'I can't come back Scott. None of us can.'

'But I've got the power, I can –'

'No, Scott.'

His dad cut him off with that same stern voice he used whenever Scott needed pulling back in line. Softening his tone, he started to explain:

'If you try and bring me back, you'll destroy everything that you've done. If the Dead Ways are opened – even to bring just one life back, it will unleash the army of the dead that is waiting here. You can't let that happen.'

He looked at Scott through shining eyes.

'The Brothers of Albion are still trying to open the Dead Ways. You've got to stop them before the winter solstice comes.'

Scott felt the tears rolling down his face. He'd come so far and now his dad was telling him that he had to go back.

'You know what you have to do,' his father said as his shadow began to slip away. 'Seal the Last Gate.'

Fighting back the tears, Scott nodded his head.

'Goodbye son.'

The outline of his father's figure was growing faint now, almost translucent in the sunlight.

'Goodbye.'

The word choked in Scott's throat as he reached out instinctively to do what he had to do. His fingers closed around the edge of the black disc and, with a single sweeping motion, his hand dragged the sun above the horizon.

For a moment, he was lost in the dazzling light, falling towards the glittering void. Then an orange sliver of light rose over the Heel Stone as the sun began its long climb over Stonehenge. A raking beam of light pierced the monument, sweeping across Scott's pale face as he lay crumpled motionless against the stone. Where the sunlight touched his skin, there was no longer any wound and Scott's mouth fell open to take the first breath of a new day.

Scott slowly pulled himself to his feet. Stepping over Buchanan's crumpled form, he turned back towards the long barrow, slowly leaving the broken circle of stones behind. The Ankou was gone, destroyed at the border of the Dead Ways, but as Scott stumbled back across the Salisbury Plain, his heart still ached. The memory of his father's face shone in his mind.

Reaching the long barrow, Scott rested his hand against its entrance, the hard chalk still cold beneath his fingers even as the rising sun warmed the sky. He stepped forward into the shadows, the ground sloping away as walked towards the heart of the tomb to find his friends. In the darkness, Scott's steely blue eyes were fixed in a resolute gaze. His father had told him what he had to do and he wouldn't let him down. He had to close the Dead Ways for ever.

END OF BOOK TWO